CENTER MASS

CENTER MASS

THE SILENCER SERIES
BOOK 20

MIKE RYAN

WWW.MIKERYANBOOKS.COM

1

It was just after lunchtime, and Recker and Haley were bringing food back into the office. They ran out to the local delicatessen to eat some sandwiches. As they started setting stuff on the counter, Recker glanced over at Jones and noticed he seemed engrossed in something.

Jones was leaning forward on the desk, his elbow resting on it, with his hand over his mouth. That was always a look of intrigue. And it usually meant something was happening that Jones had to get a handle on. Up to that point, they had nothing on the agenda. Though Jones usually had a few situations he was monitoring at any given moment, nothing was imminent.

"Something going on?" Recker asked.

Jones either didn't hear him or was so focused on what he was looking at that he didn't want to lose his concentration by responding. Recker and Haley looked at each other, getting the feeling their afternoon was about to pick up.

"Should I bother to make something?" Haley asked.

Recker shrugged. "Can always eat it on the way."

"Maybe he's playing solitaire."

Recker smiled. "Or the snake game. That's a good one."

"For your information, I was doing neither," Jones said.

"Oh, well, look at that. He speaks. Now that you're not preoccupied, should we be getting ready to leave?"

"Not at the moment."

Haley started making his sandwich. "Guess I have time, after all."

"Should we ask what's going on?" Recker said.

"A robbery just went down," Jones replied.

As Recker waited for more, it didn't appear as if it were coming. Jones looked back at his computer. Recker stood there, then eventually threw his hands up. He wasn't in the mood to play the guessing game today. Or ask fifty questions to get an idea of what was happening. If it was important, Jones would eventually spill it. And if it wasn't, it wasn't worth thinking about.

"This is good ham," Haley said.

"Told you it was good. Can't believe you never ate here before."

"I think we need to start looking into this," Jones said.

"We're already looking at it," Recker said. "The ham is good. We got some turkey too. And some bologna. Which do you want?"

"I didn't mean the food. I'm talking about this situation."

Recker raised an eyebrow. "Oh. You mean the situation you haven't told us about?"

"Maybe it's the mysterious robbery," Haley said.

Recker snapped his fingers. "Perhaps. Maybe it's the James gang. Or Bonnie and Clyde?"

"Or Dillinger."

"Good one."

"OK, OK, you two have had your fun," Jones said. "Can we get back to the real business at hand?"

"David, you haven't told us any business at hand," Recker replied.

Jones gave him a strange face. "I told you a robbery went down."

Recker glanced at Haley. "I don't know about you, but I'm pretty sure a ton of robberies go down in this city every day. I don't think that's really news, is it?"

"I guess it would depend on the circumstances," Haley answered. "A bank is big news. A liquor store. A jewelry store. That's pretty big news. A newsstand might not qualify."

"Do they even have those anymore?"

"Pretty sure they're only in shopping malls by the food court."

"Are you two done?" Jones asked.

Recker looked at his other partner again. "I don't know. Are we?"

Haley shrugged as he took a bite of his sandwich. "I don't have anything else."

"I guess we're done, then."

"There's a situation that bears watching," Jones said.

"Oh, nice. Are we going to watch it with one eye or two?"

Jones just peered over at him. "Sarcasm will get you nowhere, Michael."

Recker curled his bottom lip. "Maybe. Gotten me this far, though."

"Are you ready to hear about this or not? Or should I talk to our pretend dog?"

"We have a pretend dog? Why is this the first I'm hearing about this?" He glanced at Haley. "Did you know about this?"

"I definitely did not," Haley said.

"Is it a German Shepherd? A Lab? A Boxer? Oh, how about a Poodle?"

Jones took a deep breath, then looked up at the ceiling. "Why do I bother some days?"

Recker tapped his partner on the arm. "We didn't stop for dog treats."

"I can go back out and get some," Haley replied.

Jones lowered his head, clasped his hands together, and put them on the desk in front of him. It looked like he was praying.

"You good over there?" Recker asked.

Jones didn't reply.

"David?"

"Oh, don't worry about me," he finally said. "I'm just wondering to myself how we suddenly became a comedy club."

Recker and Haley started laughing, knowing they were getting to their friend. It helped to break up and loosen the tension that their lives were usually filled with.

"OK, let's be done with all the jokes and stuff," Recker said. "Why don't you tell us what's going on?"

Jones wasn't quite sure he believed that his friends were done with the jokes. They would often say that, then come back with another line or quip. He looked at them with a distrustful eye.

"There is a..."

Jones didn't finish, half-expecting to be interrupted. Both Recker and Haley, though, had food in their mouths.

"As I was saying, there is a string of robberies that has gone down over the last five weeks. Number three was today."

"What kind of robberies?" Recker asked.

"Diamonds."

Recker raised an eyebrow. "OK. That is pretty big news."

"And the third one recently went down today."

"Why is this the first I'm hearing about it?"

"A lot of things go on in this city, Michael. We can't be kept abreast of everything. Especially when we're already on other things. Not to mention that these things never appeared on our radar."

"OK, so we already know they're not communicating through text or email."

"Or just not saying anything dumb through them," Haley said.

"Three robberies in five weeks. That's a pretty good haul so far."

"How big are these scores?"

"From what I can gather so far, their take is about a hundred thousand dollars so far," Jones answered.

"How many people are we dealing with?" Recker asked.

"Preliminary indications are three people. Doesn't mean there couldn't be others though, too."

"Could also be a driver, maybe a lookout, or someone behind the scenes."

Jones made a couple facial expressions as he dug further into the situation. He was uncovering more fascinating information.

"What else?" Recker said.

"It appears the value has gone up in each of the three robberies. First one was worth about twenty thousand. Second one was thirty. And this one today was worth about fifty."

"Increasing each time."

"According to reports, it also seems they did not grab everything they could have. Strange."

"What do you mean?"

"There was other jewelry around that they did not take. They did not even take all the diamonds that were being stored at these places. Very odd."

"First one or two were trial runs," Haley said. "Getting the lay of the land. Making sure they had everything worked out. Everyone doing what they were supposed to. That's why it keeps increasing."

Recker nodded. "They're getting more comfortable."

"And experienced."

"But why leave money on the table?" Jones asked. "Why not take everything while you're there?"

"Maybe they were nervous about being caught," Haley said.

Recker continued to agree with his partner's assessment, snapping his fingers and pointing at him. "They were on a time limit. They gave themselves five minutes, ten minutes, whatever it was, and once that was up, they were out, regardless of how much they got or what was left."

"Smart. That's how a lot of criminals get tripped up. They get greedy."

"These guys are getting in and out before the police

show up. Do you know how long these robberies took?"

"I do not have that information currently," Jones replied.

"I'm sure it's not long."

"I'm sure it's not either," Recker said. "Probably taking what they can get within five minutes and splitting."

"Instantly makes them smarter than most."

"A little intelligence is a dangerous thing. No idea on who these guys are? Any calling cards left or anything?"

Jones shook his head. "Not as of yet. Police have no leads that I can tell. All wore hoods and masks, dark clothing, pants, long-sleeve shirts, automatic rifles."

"Making sure they don't have any visible marks to be identified."

"Due to the lack of clues, they are believed to be a professional crew."

"So we're not dealing with amateurs."

"Maybe," Haley said, not so sure himself. "The increasing scores still indicate they might have just been practicing with their first couple."

"Not necessarily, though. Could just be coincidence or how it worked out."

"Yeah, could be."

"But can't be discounted either," Recker said. "All options are on the table right now."

"What about the getaway cars?"

"Nothing there, either," Jones answered. "In two of them, the car wasn't even seen. And in this latest one, it was described as a black sedan."

"Probably stolen, anyway," Recker said.

"Most likely. In any case, there was no license plate noticed, and cameras lost sight of it within a few minutes."

"So they still had a plan for after they left these places."

"Yeah, not like the usual robbers, who just try to go as fast and as far away as possible."

"I assume all three of these places were jewelry stores?" Recker asked.

"That is correct," Jones replied. "All three were in shopping centers or strip malls."

"Any indication on whether these guys are gonna strike again?" Haley asked.

"No reason not to," Recker said. "They haven't had a close call yet. And they haven't gotten enough money to be satisfied."

"Not that I'm necessarily disagreeing, but what makes you think they're not satisfied?" Jones asked.

"Well look at the total on what they've got. A hundred thousand. Sounds like a big number. But once you start breaking it down, it's not so big. Split three ways, that's a little over thirty-three thousand each. And that's if there's only three of them. If you think there's a getaway driver, now you're down to twenty-five."

"Or someone behind the scenes," Haley said.

"Now you're down to twenty. If you've got an inside contact somewhere, they've gotta be paid. If you're selling them to someone else, you're not likely to get dollar for dollar. If you've got a third party you're selling them through, that's another expense."

"So what you're telling me is that they're basically in the red?" Jones said.

Recker smirked. "Certainly could seem that way, couldn't it? So if you assume there's five of them, you're down to ten to fifteen thousand each. But even if it winds up being just the three, you've still got the fence, and the discounted value for selling, so it's definitely not going to be enough to live on."

"Which means they're not done."

Recker shook his head. "They're not done. Not by a long shot."

2

As the team started digging into the situation a little more, they tried to see if they could see a pattern. Maybe if the robbed stores were in a certain location, they'd be able to narrow things down a little more. Unfortunately, there was no pattern that they could see. All three stores were in completely different areas.

"No discernible pattern," Jones said.

"And nobody was hurt in any of these, right?" Recker asked.

"Not a soul."

Recker continued looking at the information on his screen concerning the robberies. He was hoping that something would jump out at him, scream at him that he was overlooking something obvious. It wasn't the case, though. He leaned back in his chair.

"There's nothing here."

"We're just gonna have to wait until they hit again," Haley said.

"Problem with that is... if they're as careful, and as good, as they were the first three times, we won't hear about it until they're long gone."

"Not if they make a mistake leading up to it."

"You mean like texting each other about what robbery they're gonna do?"

"Something like that."

"Didn't do that the first three times. Or they're talking in some kind of code so that our system doesn't pick it up."

"People get complacent," Haley said. "Especially once they start having success. Start thinking it's always gonna be like that."

"Yeah, but I'm not sure we can count on that."

"What we need are ears on the street," Jones said.

Recker shot his partner a look. It was rare that Jones made such a declaration.

"Strange coming from you. You're always about the tech world. Everything can be found out online."

"And I still believe that in most cases."

"But not this one?" Recker asked.

"Even I can admit there are instances where you need eyes and ears on the street to uncover certain things. Mostly in the infancy stages of something, where there is not yet enough information to deduce a conclusion about the evidence you've uncovered. A computer cannot digest anything if there is no data that they can pull from. In this case, no computer system can pull information from thin air. We need a starting point."

Recker nodded, agreeing with the sentiment.

"Unfortunately, we don't really have eyes and ears on the street anymore," Haley said. "Tyrell's mostly retired. And we've never found a replacement."

"We've never looked that hard, either."

"Well, we tried with..." Haley snapped his fingers. "What's his name? Anyway, that didn't work out so well."

Recker sighed. "It's hard to duplicate that with someone else. Tyrell just kind of fell into my lap. It wasn't like we advertised for the job and his application stood out from all the other candidates."

"Maybe we should have Tyrell help screen."

"He knew the last guy we tried too. Like you said, that didn't work out so well."

To be truthful, not only did they not have luck with the last person Tyrell recommended, they were all pretty gun-shy about bringing another person into the fold. Though none of them verbally said it, having another situation like they had with Phillips was still fresh in their minds. And even though an informant like Tyrell wouldn't be directly working with them every day, showing up at the office, watching their backs in a dangerous situation, it was still a new person they'd have to develop trust and chemistry with. It was hard to do that now. They tried it with Phillips and it went up in flames. Tyrell recommended someone and it didn't work out. They were hesitant to try it again. Even if it was a good idea.

"Vincent?" Haley asked.

Recker shook his head. "Jewelry store robberies aren't exactly what Vincent's known for. He doesn't really play in that world. I don't think he'll have any more of an idea than we do."

"Well we gotta do something. Unless we just wait."

Recker didn't like any strategy that was available to them. But there were no good options. They had nothing. But they weren't likely to acquire anything either. He hated feeling like they were helpless, basically trapped until the robbers struck again somewhere. But that seemed to be the situation they were in.

"We just don't have enough data," Jones said. "We need a break. Maybe I can keep digging and find something we've overlooked."

Recker was skeptical of that happening.

"Maybe we should start running ex-cons that have been released in the last year," Haley said. "See if any of them have a penchant for this kind of stuff. Start tracking their movements."

It was an option, but Recker felt like that looking for a needle in a haystack. And it could be a whole lot of wasted time. Of course, it was better than sitting on their hands. Haley could see his partner wasn't too keen on the idea.

"What other options do we got?"

"Not many," Recker answered. He stood up, looking like he had something else in mind, though. "Why don't you start working on that."

"What are you going to do?"

"We need eyes and ears on the street. I'm gonna see if anyone's heard anything."

"Where?"

"Well, we have some friends and acquaintances, working bars, and clubs, and things like that. Maybe someone was there, said something, heard something, even if they didn't know what it was about at the time. Never know."

"Talk about the needle in the haystack."

Recker threw his hands up. "Yeah. No sense in us both staying here, though. Might as well kill two birds at the same time."

"You mean two needles."

Recker smiled. "Yeah."

After leaving the office, Recker spent the next few hours going around the city, checking in with a bunch of different businesses that he was friendly with. They were usually people that he helped at one time or another, either saving them at work from an unpleasant situation, or a personal problem that he showed up to help them solve. They were people that were grateful for his presence and told him if he ever needed something, they were there.

Unfortunately, they were mostly just normal people. They weren't involved in the underworld. And they usually didn't know of anything nefarious going on. But they did work in places with a high concentration of people. That sometimes led to hearing something that maybe they shouldn't have. That's what Recker had to hope for in this instance.

Over the next few hours, Recker met with twelve people. He got the same answer from all of them. None of them had heard anything about any diamond robberies. They weren't around anyone who mentioned anything mysterious that would make them think twice about what they were into.

It wasn't unexpected. But it sure didn't help any. Recker had to try something else. He didn't know what that was yet. There was always Vincent. He seemed to have contacts everywhere. But he didn't want to always lean on the crime boss. Especially if it wasn't completely necessary. He called back to the office to check on their progress.

"How are you making out?" Haley asked.

"Complete dud on my end. Nobody's heard of anything."

"That stinks."

"Yeah, but predictable, I suppose. What about you?"

"I've got a list of cons, starting to run them down."

"Anything promising yet?"

"A few things worth checking on. I'd hesitate to say anything is promising at this point."

"Figured as much."

"Coming back to the office?"

"Yeah, soon," Recker replied.

Haley could tell by his face that something else seemed to be on his friend's mind. "What else are you thinking about?"

Recker shook his head as he looked away from the camera. "I don't know. Just seems like maybe we're missing something."

"Like what?"

"I don't know. That's what I can't figure out. Seems like there should be another way to go about this, but I'm not putting my finger on what it is."

"I don't see what that would be."

"I don't know either," Recker said. "Maybe I'll call Tyrell, shoot the breeze with him."

"Hoping to coax him out of retirement?"

"No. I wouldn't do that. Maybe he's got an idea. Something we're not grasping."

"Worth a shot, I suppose."

They hung up, then Recker immediately called Tyrell, who picked up right away.

"Hey, what's going on, man?"

Recker smiled. "Just seeing how you were doing."

"Everything's good here. Just bought another truck. Hired another driver. Business is booming."

"Glad to hear it. You've worked hard for it."

"Yeah. So what's on your mind?"

"Just wanted to run something past you. Maybe you've got some ideas on how to proceed. You alone?"

"Yeah, just sitting in my office here. The door's closed, so you're good. Whatcha got?"

"A string of diamond thefts. Three in the past five weeks."

"What's the MO?"

"Don't have one right now," Recker answered. "No leads, no clues."

"Got nothing?"

Recker shook his head. "Not a thing. Police don't have anything, we don't have anything. Have the plate of a stolen car, that's it. Three men went inside the buildings. Masks, dark clothing, nothing to identify any of them."

"Man, sounds like a tough one."

"Yeah."

"What's the take?"

"About a hundred thousand in total."

"So it's likely they're gonna strike again."

"That's what we figure," Recker said.

"Any bodies dropped?"

"No. And they left things behind. In and out in five minutes regardless of how much they'd taken or how much was still there. Left gold in all three cases."

"So there were still some diamonds left behind?"

"Yeah."

"And did they take any gold at all?"

"Not that's been reported."

"Hmm. That's interesting."

"What's it say to you?"

"Professional crew," Tyrell said. "They're disciplined. Only getting what they want, or what they're told, not bothering with other stuff that doesn't interest them. Have a specific plan. In and out. Not greedy. Making sure they're not caught by waiting too long, trying to get all they can. Smart. They got their stuff together."

"And they covered themselves up head to toe so nobody could see a mark or tattoo or anything."

"Yeah, this ain't no ragtag outfit you're looking for. These guys ain't amateurs. You got your work cut out for you."

"Any ideas on where to begin, considering we've got nothing to start with? What about the fact they left gold behind? They only took diamonds. That mean anything to you?"

"Yeah, it might. Says to me you're looking for someone who deals exclusively in diamonds. That's their bag. That's their specialty."

"Someone in the crew or someone higher up?" Recker asked.

"I'd say you're looking for an independent dealer that hired a crew."

"What makes you think that?"

"They were hired to get diamonds. That's it. An independent crew that's working for themselves, they'd take whatever valuables they could get within whatever time frame they were working with. Diamonds, gold, pearls, fur, whatever. You got five minutes, you take whatever you can get your hands on, it don't matter what. You can fence it all later if it's valuable enough. But the fact that it was only diamonds tells me there's someone up top pulling the strings."

"Unless the head guy is part of the crew."

"Yeah, I guess that's possible. I can't speak to that. But there's definitely someone with a diamond specialty involved here. No doubt of that."

"Any ideas who that someone might be?" Recker asked. "Let's assume there's someone up top pulling the strings. Who would be most likely?"

"Well, it's been a while since I dealt with any of these people, man, so I might be giving you out-of-date information, you know?"

"I'm good with it. Even bad information might lead somewhere."

"There's a few guys that deal with diamonds exclusively."

"I'm assuming we're not talking about legitimate people here?"

"Who's to say who's legitimate?"

"Fair point, I guess."

"Give me an hour or so," Tyrell said. "I'll write down a list of names and send them over to you. Not all of them are local, though."

"How far is not local? We're not talking about Europe or something are we?"

"Nah. A couple are in New York. One's in Boston. A couple in Jersey. And a couple here."

"OK. Not too far, I suppose. What do you think these diamonds are being stolen for? Personal collection? Or just to sell to the highest bidder?"

"Well, if they're not well known, they're most likely being sold."

"Where are they most likely going?"

"Probably overseas. Europe. Asia. South America. It ain't likely they're staying in the country."

"And this list of names... you think they might be good for it?"

"Oh, man, they all got a reputation for being shady as all get-out. They're not tough as in Vincent-tough, but they're all sneaky. Don't take any of them for granted if you come across them. They won't be able to take you out themselves, but they'll sure as hell hire someone to do it if you cross them."

"Good thing to remember."

"All right, I gotta get a truck loaded, but as soon as I'm done that, I'll send that list over."

"Thanks, I appreciate it."

"No worries. Hey, you're gonna have to get yourself a new Tyrell soon. I mean, every day that passes, more goes on, stuff happens, I become less useful."

"Yeah. Easier said than done, though."

"Don't I know it? Not easy to replace the o-riginal."

"Maybe one day someone will just fall into my lap."

"Not likely, though."

"No. Not likely."

3

B y the time Recker got back to the office, he had a message on his phone from Tyrell. He wrote down the list of names, and took a picture of it to send to Recker. As Recker walked into the office, neither of his friends bothered to even take a glance at him. They were deep into their own work, not that much was coming from it.

Recker sat down at the desk and started writing down the names Tyrell sent him. Jones stopped typing as he noticed Recker scribbling things down.

"Something we should know about?"

"Tyrell gave me some names to check on," Recker answered. "I can work on it so you guys don't have to stray from what you're doing."

Jones rubbed his eyes. "I don't think that's much of a hindrance, to be honest. It doesn't seem I'm on the right track with anything."

"Me neither," Haley said.

"Those ex-cons?" Recker asked.

"A whole lot of nothing. I can't find anything worth pursuing. Maybe there's something there, but..."

"Let's switch lanes to this. There's seven names on here. Tyrell seems to think if there's someone pulling the strings, these are the most likely candidates."

Both Jones and Haley glanced at the names as Recker wrote them down. None of them were familiar, though. Definitely nobody they had ever crossed paths with before.

"I can start running these down," Jones said. "But what if there's someone new on the scene?"

Recker didn't seem bothered by the prospect. "Then one of these guys will know it. And, if they're making life difficult for these guys, they may be more likely to share in order to get them out of the picture."

"How you wanna work it?" Haley asked. "Stake out will take too long with all these candidates."

Recker agreed. "Yeah, that would take too long with so many of them. I think we've got two options. We either straight up approach each of these guys and ask them some tough questions, or we keep digging here, and hope we come across something that incriminates one of them."

"Well I know which one I'm for," Jones said.

Recker grinned. "I say we start banging down some doors."

"How did I know you would suggest that?"

"Lucky guess?"

"Fat chance."

"Running these guys down on this end is a good start," Recker said. "And it'll help to give us some background info about who we're dealing with. But I'm not sure we're gonna find out who's behind this unless we get out there."

"Besides, if we were gonna uncover some decoded messages or secret texts or something, wouldn't we have them already?" Haley asked.

"Not if they were speaking in code," Jones replied. "Remember, the system only picks up specific words. Rob, steal, assault, murder, you know the rest. If they're not speaking in those terms, the system will not detect it. So if they say, 'let's go shopping on Thursday', and that's code for let's go rob the place, we won't get an alert on it. There's no way to pick that up."

"So what's the point?"

"The point is, I can start getting into the emails and phone records of these people and start figuring out if there's something there underneath the surface."

That still seemed like it would take too long for Recker's tastes. Jones could hear it from the way his partner mumbled under his breath.

"I know it's not as quick as some of us would like it. But I can't speed that up. The process is the process."

"Slow process, more like it," Recker said. "And that's all well and good. And we should definitely be doing that."

"I feel a but coming on."

Recker smiled. "But, getting into the phone records, texts, and emails is a time-consuming process. As in days and days."

"Not necessarily."

"Two of these guys are in the city. Let's get in on them first."

"And do what?" Jones asked. "You're just going to walk right up to them and ask if they're behind these diamond robberies? That's going to get you nowhere. They're obviously not going to admit to anything, whether they're involved or not."

"No, they won't."

"So what's the point of it?"

"The point is to apply pressure. If they know people are on them, maybe they'll make a mistake. Or maybe they'll dial it back. Or maybe it'll scare them off."

"To do it somewhere else?"

Recker shrugged. "I mean, we can't be everywhere. All we can do is protect where we are. If it scares them off to California or something, there's not much we can do about that. But it will protect the people here."

"Or maybe one of them knows who this gang is and thinks it's bad for business," Haley said. "That's always possible."

"But not likely," Jones said. "If they thought it were bad for business, they would probably take care of it themselves instead of ratting someone out."

"Not necessarily," Recker replied. "Why do the dirty work and heavy lifting yourself if you can just pass the word on to someone else and have them take care of it? It also leaves you out of any possible repercussions if something fails."

"Unless the gang knows they informed on them."

Recker tossed one of his hands up. "Any direction we go, there's a possible reason not to. I prefer being proactive and upping the pressure."

"I know you do. There's also always the chance that you up the pressure so much that you inadvertently start something that you're not prepared for."

"Such as?"

"Such as someone doesn't take kindly to your line of questions," Jones said. "And they immediately take some shots at you when you're not prepared for it."

Recker didn't seem worried about those prospects. He would actually welcome them.

"I'd be good with that."

Jones rolled his eyes. "Somehow, I knew you would say that."

"Hey, if we get them riled up to the point where they come after us, then we don't have to keep looking or investigating. Then we know we got our guy."

"Assuming they haven't killed you first."

Recker smirked. "I like my chances."

"You are not invincible, you know. I know you like to think that you're better than everyone else out there in terms of getting into a fight, but you can be beaten."

"I know that. I don't think I'm invincible. But I do think I'm smart. And I'm not oblivious to what's going on out there."

"I already know you're going to do what you want, I just want to make sure you think of all the possibilities before you walk into one of these meetings."

"Always do," Recker said.

Jones was resigned to losing the battle. "Then I guess we should find out where these people are."

Jones typed the names into the computer, and after a few minutes, identified their first targets. Since two of the names were in the city, they were the first options.

"Charles D'Amonico. Forty-one years old. Major importer and exporter. Owns several businesses. Married. Two kids, both teenagers. Looks like he's been the subject of several criminal probes by the authorities in the last few years, though nothing appears to have stuck. It seems as though he's currently in the clear."

"Who's the second guy?" Recker asked.

"The second name is Damien Vervaat. Not currently married. One ex-wife. No kids. Thirty-two years old. Deals in jewelry. Arrested for receiving stolen goods."

"Looks like two good candidates," Haley said.

Recker nodded. "Yeah. Whether they're the candidates we're looking for remains to be seen. Let's grab their addresses and figure out the best time to strike."

"Strike?" Jones asked.

"Figure of speech. Best time to ask questions."

Jones gave him a dubious eye. "I'm not sure barging into their homes would be wise."

"Nobody said anything about barging into their homes. Place of business would be fine. Unless they're not there."

Jones made a noise as he looked at the screen.

"Something wrong?" Recker asked.

"Uh, no. No. Nothing wrong."

"Then what'd you make that noise for?"

"Well it appears Mr. Vervaat just posted something on one of his social media accounts."

"I assume there's something interesting about that?"

"He posted a picture of the front of Mona Ray's."

"Mona Ray's?" Haley asked. "Isn't that a restaurant or something?"

Recker nodded. "Yeah. Fancy place, if I recall."

"That's the one," Jones said. "His post says, 'always look forward to eating at my favorite restaurant'."

"That means he's there now."

"So it would appear."

Recker looked at his partner. "You hungry?"

Haley patted his stomach. "I suppose I could throw something down."

As the two men started to get ready, Jones hoped to caution them slightly.

"I do not know if he's with anyone. Whether that be

guards, a companion, business associates, or whatever. You're walking into this blind."

"Wouldn't be the first time," Recker said.

Before leaving, Recker and Haley walked back over to the computer to get another look at Vervaat's face.

"Send that picture to me," Recker said.

Jones nodded. "Done. Please be careful. I would assume a man like this is not traveling alone, or without some sort of protection."

"Doesn't matter what kind of protection he's got. It won't protect him from us."

4

Recker and Haley got out of their car once they parked, and walked toward the front door of the Mona Ray.

"Ever been to this place before?" Haley asked.

Recker looked at the bright yellow sign at the top of the building. "Nope. Can't say that I have."

"Popular spot, I've heard. Must be good."

"Just because it's expensive, and popular, doesn't make it good."

"That's true."

"Plus, aren't most of these fine dining places like a hundred dollars a plate?"

"On the cheap end."

Recker chuckled. "Yeah. On the cheap end. A hundred to two hundred a plate and it's usually not even enough to fill up a bird."

Haley laughed. "I don't know. I think that's a myth. I'm pretty sure they give you more than that."

"Guess it depends on the plate. I know I've definitely seen pictures of like... one chicken nugget with a leaf over top of it and they call it a day."

"Go to a lot of fine dining places, do you?"

"Oh yeah. Mia and I go to one every Tuesday and Friday night like clockwork. Didn't you know?"

"No, I somehow missed that."

"Not quite my style."

They reached the front door. Once they went inside, they were immediately greeted by a host. The man looked a little dismayed that neither of the two men appeared to be wearing the proper attire. Neither were wearing suits, which was usually a requirement.

"Uh, can I help you two gentlemen?"

Recker and Haley glanced at each other, suddenly realizing it was one of those types of places. They would have to improvise.

"Yes, we're expected," Haley said. "Our friend has a change of clothes for us once we go in."

"Oh. Very well. What's the name?"

Haley walked next to the host to check out the names in his book, leaving the man distracted, and letting Recker slip in unnoticed.

"Chuck Clark," Haley said.

Recker started walking around the restaurant, eventually finding Damien Vervaat sitting at a table to the rear of the room. He was sitting across from another man. It was unclear from Recker's position as to whether it was a business or personal meeting. Recker quickly scanned the area, looking for signs of a bodyguard. All the other tables in the vicinity were filled up, all with couples of two or four seated around them. Except for one table.

That table had two men sitting there. But it was obvious they were not a romantic couple. They weren't sitting next to or across from each other. They were sitting diagonally from the other. While they were eating their food, their heads were down, looking at their phones, and there was no conversation, or even a glance between the two of them. There was no doubt these were the guards. They also looked the part. They were on the younger side, in their twenties, most likely, and on the bigger side. They had the muscular look to them.

But it wasn't a deterrent to Recker. He knew he had Haley coming at some point as soon as he ditched the host. So now was as good a time as any to introduce himself.

Recker walked right up to the table and sat down between the two men, inching his chair over towards Vervaat. The look the two men were giving the stranger was priceless.

"Excuse me..." Vervaat said.

"No, there's no excuses for you," Recker replied.

"Excuse me?"

"What'd I just say? Put your listening ears on."

"Who do you think you are?!"

"Well, I'll tell you."

Recker didn't get the chance, as he could see two men standing behind him out of the corner of his eye. He knew it was the two goons making their presence known.

"Throw him out of here," Vervaat said. "And don't be gentle about it."

Recker put his hand up to stop any festivities from happening. "Now, now, that's not nice. And I wouldn't do that."

"And why is that?"

"Probably because the guy behind them will put a hole through each of them if they try it."

Vervaat looked on in horror as he noticed the man behind his two guards, who also turned around. Haley didn't have a gun visible since they were in a high-profile restaurant, but he'd make the implication clear enough.

"I don't wanna drop anybody right here," Haley said. "As long as everyone keeps a cool head, everything will be just fine."

"What do you people want?" Vervaat asked.

"Tell your guards to sit down and I'll tell you," Recker said. "We're just going to have a conversation, you and I. That's it. Nobody's going to get hurt. Nobody needs to get roughed up. We talk, and then we leave, and you get to enjoy the rest of your dinner."

Vervaat certainly didn't look pleased, but appeared

to know the other men had the upper hand for the moment. He looked back at his men and waved them off. They went back to their own table. Haley joined them, sitting at the end of it to make sure they behaved nicely.

"Now what is this about?" Vervaat asked.

"First of all, it's a little early for dinner, isn't it?" Recker asked, looking at his watch. "I mean, it's barely after four o'clock. My grandparents don't even eat dinner this early."

"If it's any of your business, I'm hungry. I haven't eaten all day."

"Oh. Oh. Well that makes sense."

"If you're done questioning my eating habits, once again I'll ask, what is this about?"

Recker put his elbow on the table to start talking, then stopped and looked back at the other man.

"Is it safe to talk business in front of him? Is he a business partner, a date, what?"

"I don't think that's any of your concern!"

"No, maybe not. I'd just hate for you to lose a prospective client, or a late-night romp in the hay because of what we discuss here. But if it's all the same to you..."

Vervaat took a deep sigh, looking more displeased than ever. He looked at the man across from him and raised his hand off the table.

"If you would... I'm so sorry about this."

The man stood up. "No, it's OK."

"I'll make it up to you later."

"Call me."

As the man walked away from the table, Recker smiled at Vervaat. "That was nice."

Vervaat gave him a scowl. "I think I have been rather agreeable and pleasant here considering the circumstances. But that only lasts for so long. Now, for the last time, who are you, and what do you want?"

"Well, as far as who I am, some people call me The Silencer. Friends call me something else. You can call me Mr. Silencer."

Vervaat raised his left eyebrow, the name obviously ringing a bell with him.

"I can see you've heard of me."

"I seem to recall hearing the name a time or two," Vervaat said.

"Good. Then you obviously know of my reputation."

Knowing that reputation, Vervaat's demeanor seemed to suddenly change. Instead of being angry and defiant, his tone shifted to a more pleasant attitude.

"What is it that I can do for you?"

"Well, since you asked nicely, I was wondering if you could tell me anything about the string of diamond robberies that have occurred lately?"

"What string of diamond robberies?"

"You know, there's been three of them in five weeks. Don't tell me you know nothing about them. Especially considering you deal in jewelry for a living, and you've been arrested before for receiving stolen goods."

A small grin crept over the corner of Vervaat's mouth. He could appreciate that Recker did his homework on him. He took a sip of his wine.

"So I deal in jewelry. That doesn't mean I have the faintest idea about these robberies you speak of."

"Are you going to tell me you know nothing about them? This is your business. It's what you do. I'd imagine something like that is pretty big in your world."

"Maybe I've heard something about it. That doesn't mean I know what's going on. And as far as the stolen goods thing, that was a complete misunderstanding."

"Oh, I'm sure. You had no idea the goods were stolen, right?"

"That's correct. So if that will be all...?"

"That will not be all," Recker replied. "I don't believe you."

"Well that's not my problem."

Recker leaned forward, making sure his tone was received loud and clear. "Well you better make it your problem. Because when I start looking into something, people start winding up in a not-so-nice position. Whether they're involved or not. Especially people on the wrong side of the law. I'm sure you get my drift."

"I do. And I don't respond well to threats."

"I guess that makes two of us. Just so you know, I'm

coming after this hard. And when I find out who's involved, they're gonna fall harder."

"I wish them luck," Vervaat said.

Recker smiled. "They're gonna need it."

"Once again, I am completely in the dark about the topic of which you're inquiring."

Recker could see he wasn't going to get anything out of the man. At least not right now. But he accomplished what he wanted. He got a feel for Vervaat. And now the man knew Recker was coming, assuming Vervaat was involved in these robberies. And if he wasn't, it wouldn't hurt for Vervaat to think Recker was watching his business. Maybe it'd keep him on the straight and narrow for a little bit.

"OK," Recker said. "I guess that will do it for now."

Recker reached his hand across the table, acting like he was going to shake hands. Instead, his hand hit the wine glass in front of Vervaat, knocking it over, and spilling the wine across the man's lap.

"Oh, I'm so sorry. Some days I just don't know how clumsy I am."

Vervaat slightly stood up, looking at his guest, with contempt in his eyes. He then sat back down, though he still didn't look happy.

"I'm sure we'll be seeing each other again," Recker said.

"I'm sure."

Recker stood up and walked away from the table. Haley quickly followed, though he also kept an eye on the two guards to make sure that they didn't follow him. They didn't. Once they were outside, they walked back to their car.

"What did you think?"

"Oh, he's a weasel, all right," Recker said.

"Yeah, but is he the weasel we're looking for?"

"I don't know. That's the question. He could be. But he didn't say anything to make me believe it yet. We'll just have to wait and see. I lit a fire in there. Now we have to see if it explodes."

5

While they waited on something further to follow up on with Vervaat, Recker and Haley turned their attention to the next name on the list. Charles D'Amonico. Jones was keeping an eye on Vervaat, seeing if Recker's conversation with the man spurred something on. But in the meantime, D'Amonico was having a big birthday celebration for one of his kids. It was a big event at a country club.

Recker and Haley pulled into the parking lot, a little surprised at the ease of entry. They assumed with someone of D'Amonico's background, there would have been some kind of security around. Not that they were upset at being able to go in without having to figure out a plan.

"Some people make it too easy," Haley said.

"Letting whoever wants to come in, I guess."

"Not only that, but advertising where you'll be all

the time. Social media, man. Especially people like this, who undoubtedly has made some enemies along the way, just announces when and where he'll be, no care in the world. They don't even try to hide anymore."

"People don't realize how vulnerable they can make themselves," Recker said.

"I guess it's better for us. I mean, we could find out anyway, but it's easier when you just come out and tell us. Cuts out all the games."

"Yeah. Used to be you had to dig for a lot of this information. I mean, people like us could still find it, but it'd take a day or two, if not more. Now, people just flat out post things they really should keep to themselves."

"It's the culture we live in. Everybody wants to be famous."

They walked into the club, still surprised that nobody stopped them and asked if they belonged there. They didn't see a guard, or anybody that looked like they worked in security. But there were a large number of people there. It had to be at least three or four hundred.

"Imagine having this big of a party for your fifteenth birthday?"

"Kind of makes you wonder what they'll do for sixteen," Recker replied.

"Probably buy them a car. A new one."

"Wouldn't doubt it."

It was a big event, with a ton of people, and a lot of space to cover. Recker and Haley started moving through the throngs of people. They soon realized their initial estimate was low. Much too low. They quickly figured out the room they were in was only a small part of the event. There were even more people outside.

Since they were there, they went over to a table and made themselves a drink, and a sandwich. They didn't have to be in a hurry. This party wasn't breaking up anytime soon. They stood near the wall and just watched, hoping they'd get a glimpse of D'Amonico soon enough. They figured he'd have to come into their view at some point. Even by accident.

They waited for about half an hour until something finally broke for them. Someone in the other corner of the room got on a microphone, and throngs of people started crowding the room from the outside. Then music started playing. Recker put a finger in his ear and scrunched his nose. He usually wasn't a fan of the club-style music that blared out at ungodly decibels.

A DJ got on the microphone and started talking, and people started moving around, leaving the center of the room open for dancing.

"You wanna try your hand?" Recker asked.

"Are you offering?"

Recker laughed. "See if you can pick out someone single."

"Not sure this is my crowd."

Recker then tapped his friend on the arm and pointed to the far end of the room. He caught a glimpse of their target.

"There he is. See him?"

"Yeah, I got him," Haley answered. "Guess we should introduce ourselves."

Recker and Haley moved around dozens of people in their way, eventually making their way over to a table where there were different drinks set up. D'Amonico was oblivious to the men making their way toward him. He just poured himself a glass of alcohol when Recker and Haley reached him.

"Wondering if we could go outside?" Recker said.

D'Amonico quickly sized the two men up, not liking what he was seeing. "I'm sorry?"

Recker pointed to himself and Haley. "Us." He then pointed to D'Amonico. "You." He then pointed to the door. "Outside."

"What for?"

"Because we have things to discuss."

"We do? Do I know you?"

"No, but we know you."

"How did you get in here?"

"Just walked right in," Recker said. "Your security is pretty light. Surprising for a guy like you."

"You can't be here."

D'Amonico tried to walk through the middle of the

two men, but they each grabbed one of his arms and held him back.

"Not a good idea," Recker said. "If you want, we can get on the microphone and start talking about some of the things you're into and ruin your nice little karaoke party you got going on here. Or you can come with us peacefully and we can have our chat, then we'll leave and you can go on with this thing like nothing ever happened."

"What are you here for?"

"Let's go outside and we can discuss it."

D'Amonico wasn't happy about it, but agreed, and turned around. He walked outside, closely followed by Recker and Haley. They bumped shoulders with a few other people as they made their way to a round table. They sat down and D'Amonico anxiously took a sip of his drink, hoping it would calm his nerves.

"Now who are you guys?"

"Let's just say we're here in public interests," Recker answered.

"Meaning?"

"Three robberies have gone down in the last five weeks. Valued at a hundred thousand."

"I don't know anything about that."

"Somehow, I figured that would be your answer."

D'Amonico shrugged. "I don't know what you're talking about."

"Nobody ever does."

"Why would I know anything about that?"

"You import and export, don't you?"

"I don't rob people."

"Not what the government says," Recker replied. "You've had several major investigations towards you."

"Towards my companies. Not me personally."

"You run them."

"There were some minor improprieties that were made by junior members of the business. That has all been rectified."

"Couldn't rectify it the first time?"

"I'm growing tired of these accusations. If you have something to say, say it to my attorney."

"We're not the police," Recker said. "We don't deal with attorneys."

"Then who are you?"

"We're a private security company and we've been asked to look into your dealings."

"My dealings? Screw off. I don't have to sit here and listen to you about anything. If you're not the authorities, take a hike. And if you don't, I'll have you forcibly removed from the property."

"Do you really think he wants to do that?" Haley asked.

"No, I don't think he does," Recker said. "I'm not sure he understands what he'd be bringing onto himself if he did."

"What is that supposed to mean?" D'Amonico said.

Recker turned his head and looked at the crowd of people. "A lot of people around here today. Also appears to be a lot of impressionable young people. Teenagers. People your kids go to school with. Do you really want those young minds thinking they're going to school, and are friends with, the children of a career criminal? Think of how that might make them feel."

"My kids are not of your concern."

"You're right. They're not. What does concern me is the fact that there are people out there taking diamonds that don't belong to them. And then reselling them. That concerns me."

"And I've already told you I have nothing to do with that."

"You can see how we'd be hesitant to believe you, right?" Recker said.

"You can believe anything you want."

A woman walked over to their table. D'Amonico tried waving her off, not wanting her to come over. She didn't recognize the signs he was trying to give her. She had a wine glass in her hand, and a smile on her face, enjoying the party. She leaned over and kissed D'Amonico on the cheek.

"Hey, Charles, who are these people? I've never met them before."

"And you won't now. Let us be."

Recker instantly smiled at the woman and reached out his hand. "Hi. We're friends of your husband's."

"No they're not."

"He's so modest," Recker said. "We're old friends, actually."

"No."

The woman was beginning to look confused, not sure what was going on.

"Do you know what your husband is involved in?" Recker asked.

"Excuse me?" Mrs. D'Amonico asked.

"Oh, I was just referring to all the criminal investigations and all that."

"That was all just a big misunderstanding. That's all been settled."

"Yeah, but usually when there's smoke, there's fire," Recker said. "I'd assume that won't be the last of your troubles."

Mrs. D'Amonico rubbed her husband's shoulders. "Honey, what is this about?"

"It's nothing, darling. Just some people here who are overstaying their welcome."

Recker kept up the pressure. "You don't happen to know anything about the diamond robberies he's involved with, do you?"

Mrs. D'Amonico looked stunned to hear the question. "What? Diamond robberies? What is this?"

"It's a lot of nonsense," her husband answered. "They're just trying to be cute. Grasping for straws and throwing darts at the wall. But nothing's going to stick here."

"I guess we'll see," Recker said.

He and Haley stood up, ready to conclude their business. They didn't expect D'Amonico to give them much. They just wanted to let him know they were there. Maybe a little extra pressure would make him make a mistake. Some people didn't operate well when they knew there were eyes watching.

"But make no mistake," Recker said, wanting to give him some lasting words to remember them by. "We're watching you. And we're coming."

6

The next morning, the team was back at the office, going over their previous two encounters. Jones had been tracking some of their movements, but nothing stuck out as interesting. Both D'Amonico and Vervaat had offices, and they both went straight there. Jones was tapping into their phone records, but he hadn't come across anything that seemed noteworthy.

"Let's keep on with the list," Recker said. "Who's next?"

Jones picked the paper up to read the names. "Kavi Sharma. Indian businessman." He went back to typing on his computer. "He's actually on a plane right now, returning from an overseas trip."

"What's his story?"

"Several arrests, no convictions. Runs the gamut of illegal activities. You name it, he's involved in it."

"Sounds like my kind of guy."

"Indeed. I would imagine we can scratch him off the list, however."

"Why's that?"

"He hasn't even been here," Jones replied. "He's been in Europe for the last week."

Recker shook his head. "Doesn't mean he's not involved. This is the internet and tech age. You can have things done from a continent away."

"In fact, that may even make him more of a candidate," Haley said. "He gave himself a nice alibi he can use."

"Definitely can."

"Well, his plane is touching down in a couple hours," Jones said.

"Where?"

"Atlantic City."

"Is he traveling with anyone?" Recker asked.

"From what I can gather, he does employ the use of guards. Whether they're traveling with him, or meeting him at the airport, I feel confident in saying you will run into them."

Recker looked at the time. Considering the plane wasn't going to land for a couple hours, and it was just a little over an hour drive from their location, they had plenty of time. They would have to think of a plan on how to separate Sharma from his guards, though. They could do it the obvious way, and just take them out by brute force if necessary, but they weren't looking for a fight at the moment. Not unless there was no other way.

They didn't take too long to think about it, wanting to get down to the airport in plenty of time before the plane landed. They'd been to the airport before, but traffic patterns there could be different depending on the day and time. They didn't love the plan they came up with, but it was better than no plan at all. But it did give them the chance to talk to Sharma peacefully. And if that didn't work, then they'd use force.

Once they arrived at Atlantic City International, Recker and Haley split up. They were both in the general area of where Sharma would be arriving. But they didn't want to be seen together. They were on the lookout, however, for men that could be assumed to be working for Sharma. They knew the type. Usually on the bigger side, maybe a scowl on their face, and had the look of a bodyguard. Most of them looked similar.

After being there for a while, and not seeing anything, and with only a few minutes until the plane arrived, Recker thought he finally picked up something. He called Haley, who he could see standing against the far wall.

"I'm seeing one," Recker said. "You got him?"

Haley instantly started scanning the area. "I'm not picking anything up."

"Look to your left. There's a mom kneeling, talking to a small child. Just beyond them there's a guy with a brown suit. Black hair."

Haley found where his partner was talking about. "Yeah, I see him."

"He's the only one I'm picking up so far."

Haley started looking around some more. To their far right, he thought he detected another one. "Hey, look to your left."

Recker turned his head. "Where?"

"Just beyond the coffee shop. Blue suit."

"I got him."

"How do you wanna work it?"

"I guess like how we planned," Recker answered. "We'll have to time it perfectly, though."

"As long as they don't detect us on the way we should be fine."

"Keep our phones out and talk as we walk out. They won't be as suspicious of people who seem preoccupied on their phones."

"Good idea."

Once the plane landed, and the passengers began getting off, they easily located Sharma, as he was greeted by one of his guards. Both Recker and Haley started walking towards the exit, before Sharma even passed them. It would give them the advantage, as Sharma wouldn't get the feeling that he was being followed. Especially if Recker and Haley were in front of him.

When they got near the exit, Recker took a quick peek behind him, just to make sure their targets were still on their way. By now, Sharma had hooked up with the second guard, as well. Recker and Haley walked out the doors, and stood along the curb. They still had their phones pressed to their ears.

They noticed Sharma exit, his two guards on each side of him. All three waited there for a moment, waiting for his car to be brought up. Once it parked along the curb, the two guards walked with Sharma, one of them opening up the back door to the sedan for him. That was the cue.

As Sharma got in, Recker and Haley rushed over to the car. Recker pushed one of the guards into the back seat, making him fall forward, landing on Sharma's lap. Recker hopped in, quickly pulling out his gun, making sure that everyone understood who had the upper hand.

As Recker was doing that, Haley kicked out the back knee of the other guard, sending him down on one leg. He then swiftly jumped into the passenger seat, and removed his gun, pointing it at the driver.

"Go," Haley said.

"Where?" the driver asked.

"Just drive. Get on the highway and don't get off."

The driver started to turn his head to look at his boss to make sure it was OK. Haley stopped that.

"Don't look at him. I'm giving you the orders. You either follow them, or you won't be around to get another."

The driver nodded, then put the car in drive.

"What's the meaning of this?" Sharma asked. "You

can't barge into my car and do whatever it is you're doing."

"Looks like we can and we did," Recker replied.

By now, the other guard in the back had dropped to the floor, facing Recker.

"Do you know who I am?" Sharma asked.

"Uh, yeah, yeah. Very intimidating and I'm shaking in my boots. Anyway, let's get down to business."

"I have no business with you."

"Well, we'll just see about that."

"You won't get away with this."

"I haven't taken anything yet," Recker said.

"Is this a robbery?"

Recker shook his head. "No."

"Kidnapping?"

"Nope."

"Then I don't understand."

"I understand you're involved in a lot of criminal activities. You don't have to deny it, and I'm not a cop, so I don't care about your response. What I am concerned about is that there's been a diamond robbery, three of them, in the last five weeks. And I got a list of names of people who might be responsible. Seven of them. And guess whose name appeared?"

"Mine?"

"Ding, ding, you're the lucky winner."

Sharma smirked. "What do I win?"

"A date with me, obviously."

"I'll pass my winnings on to someone else."

"No give backs. Anyway, I'm here to see if you know something about it?"

"I do not. I haven't even been here for the last week. So how would I know a robbery of diamonds occurred?"

Recker shrugged. "Oh, I don't know. How did you know a robbery happened in the last week?"

Sharma looked down and smiled, almost as if he were embarrassed at being caught. "I just assumed since you were here that it happened recently. Not because I have any prior knowledge of such an activity."

"Oh, I'm sure, I'm sure." Recker pointed to the guy on the floor. "What about him? What's he been up to since you were gone?"

Sharma looked at his man for a moment. "Just hanging out at the pool."

Recker grinned. "Good times, I'm sure. Just out of curiosity, what would you do if you were given a hundred thousand dollars' worth of diamonds right now? And this is a serious question to which I'd like an answer."

Sharma tilted his head up as he pondered the question. "Well I guess that would depend. How many hands are getting a piece of the action, what are the diamonds worth on the market, what kind of deal is lined up to begin with, and where are they actually going? All those things need to be accounted for."

"Suppose there's at least three people getting a piece. But maybe as high as five or six."

"Then it's not worth it. At least from my vantage point."

"Why is that?"

"Even if we say there's five people getting a piece, that's only twenty thousand dollars each. That's not even a risk I would consider worth it."

"Too light?"

Sharma nodded. "Exactly. If I'm going to risk something, it's going to be something that's big. Something worth a lot of money. But twenty thousand dollars? Why bother?"

"What if it's just a warm-up for the crew trying to pull off the job? They're working their way up to a bigger score. Each job's bigger and bigger. Maybe they're trying to work out any issues before they try for the big one. Wouldn't that then be worth it?"

Sharma looked away for a second and made a noise, indicating he was considering the question seriously.

"Interesting. I suppose in theory it's possible."

Recker could tell by the way he talked that Sharma still wasn't buying it. "But you don't think so."

"Oh, maybe if it's a small crew, that's entirely possible. Not too many hands in the pot."

"But not for a big operation like you have?"

Sharma curled his lip and shook his head. "Not a chance. What you're describing is a group that are a bunch of amateurs to start with. They have to start small until they figure out what they're doing, best practices, so on and so forth. They're continuing to work their way up until they get that big one. Then they can move on."

"And that doesn't interest you?"

"It would not."

"Why not?"

"As I said, too many risks. The more this crew goes out there, the odds increase that they're caught. They'll eventually do something stupid, they'll eventually make a mistake, they'll eventually run into a job that doesn't go off without a hitch. They'll be an off-duty cop that foils their plan, a bank or store manager that doesn't cooperate like the others, a patrol car that happens to cruise by at the wrong time, a customer who wants to play hero, or a getaway car that gets boxed in inadvertently. As you can see, each time you pull off a job, the odds increase of something going wrong. Even to the best of the bunch."

"So what would you do?" Recker asked. "Theoretically, of course. If you wanted a bunch of diamonds that someone else had."

"I would hire the most experienced crew I could find to begin with. And I'd take down the biggest score I could get. That way the risks are big enough to be worth it for everybody. A hundred thousand split five ways isn't worth it. Ten million split six or seven ways...

then I'd be more willing to talk. One job. Make it big. And make it count. And then walk away."

There was a conviction in the man's voice, and in his words. Recker got the feeling Sharma was leveling with him. Unlike the others they had talked to so far, he didn't get the sense he was being lied to. Of course, it was always possible Sharma was trying to sell him a bill of goods. But Recker didn't think so.

"I would imagine a man like you knows quite a bit about different things that are going on."

"Some might say," Sharma said.

"Perhaps you might hear something about the situation at some point. An upstart crew, someone trying to unload something valuable, someone who's operating in the shadows for some reason."

"In my business there is always someone operating in the shadows. Take yourself for example."

Recker smiled. "Yeah. I guess that's true."

"I'm afraid I cannot help you with the matter, though. I have nothing to offer. But to be clear, I'm not sure how it would benefit me even if I did."

"Well, I'm sure someone as smart as yourself understands that behavior like this brings down the heat on everybody. A one-off job, that's the end of it. But something that keeps on going on for weeks and weeks, well, that brings a lot of attention. And it brings attention to a lot of people who aren't involved. And people start looking into their business. And sometimes those people don't want extra eyeballs looking into their business. Because sometimes they have things they're hiding. And things they want to stay hidden."

Sharma rubbed his chin. "I would imagine that's true."

"Chris, take us back to the house."

Recker thought they were getting all they were going to. Not that it was much. But he at least thought they could cross one name off their list. Well, maybe put it on the bottom. He didn't think Sharma was the most likely suspect at this point.

Haley directed the driver at that point on which way to go, and eventually led him right back to the airport, just like they had planned. On the way, Recker continued grilling Sharma, wanting to see if his answers deviated at all. But they didn't. Nothing the man said indicated he'd be involved in something like this. At least not on the scale that the diamond crew was currently operating on.

They eventually pulled back up to the same exact spot as when they left. Before getting out, Recker reached into his pocket and removed one of his business cards that only had a phone number on it. He handed it to Sharma.

"Maybe if you happen to hear something you'll give me a call?"

Sharma briefly looked at the card. "Perhaps I will."

"Oh, and, uh, don't bother looking for us after we

leave here, or think that you'll find us by searching for that phone number. You won't."

Sharma smiled. "Never even crossed my mind."

"I'm sure it didn't. If everything you say is true, you'll never see us again."

"And if I was lying?"

"Then we'll be your worst nightmare."

Sharma nodded. "Understood. It was a pleasure talking to you."

"I bet."

"I never did get your name, though."

"That's because I didn't offer it."

Recker and Haley then got out of the car, and walked away like nothing had ever happened. They periodically looked back to make sure nobody was coming after them, which they couldn't discount. But nobody was.

Back inside the car, the guard had picked himself off the floor and sat on the seat.

"You want me to go after them?"

"No, let it slide," Sharma answered. He then looked at the business card.

"You're just gonna let them get away with this?"

"Get away with what? As far as I'm concerned, they did nothing wrong. They invited themselves in and we had a pleasant conversation. One that gives us much to think about."

"It does?"

"Maybe this diamond business can give us a new friend. If we play our cards right."

"Who? That guy?"

"He seems to be a man of grit and resources. You want men like that to be allies. Not enemies. Keep your ears open about this diamond business. See if we can learn anything that we can then offer our mystery man."

"Like what?"

"Who knows? But it's wise not to close any doors if they can be kept open. If we have something to trade, I'd imagine someone like that could be very useful. We must keep those options open."

"I'll start checking around."

"Good. The minute you hear something, I want to know about it." Sharma looked down at the business card again. He smiled. "Good fortune has a way of finding you when you least expect it. Always keep your doors open. That's the lesson you can learn from this. If your door is closed, you can miss out on everything. Especially... the diamond in the rough."

7

A couple more days had passed, and nothing new was learned about the diamond robberies. Recker and Haley visited some of the other names on the list, though they didn't learn anything interesting from them either. Everyone was taking the deaf, dumb, and blind approach. For people that Tyrell thought were most likely to be involved, none of them seemed to know anything about anything. Of course they knew it was an act.

And while Recker and Haley definitely had their favorites who they thought were involved, they couldn't say it with any amount of certainty. All they had right now was gut feelings. There was nothing concrete that would tie any of the seven people on the list to the robberies. But they were still digging, hoping they would find something out before the next robbery occurred.

The one thing they assumed they had was time. Not a lot of it. Definitely not something they could push to the back burner, but up to now, no robbery had occurred within ten days of another one. It wasn't much time. But they weren't up against it yet.

Recker was in the office when he saw he was getting a call from Tyrell. It was an unexpected one. Recker answered.

"Hey, I gotta make this short, as I gotta jet here real quick."

"What's up?" Recker asked.

"How you making out on that diamond thing?"

"Still working on it. Going through the leads you gave us."

"Good. Well I got one more for you."

"Yeah? What's that?"

"A contact. Says he might have some information on it."

"A contact?" Recker's internal alarms were already going off. "He contacted you out of the blue?"

Tyrell shook his head. "No, man, not like that. I put some feelers out there to some people I still talk to from time to time. Figured I'd give you some extra help if I could. A couple of them got back to me. That's all there is to it."

Recker was still skeptical. "Not that I'm ungrateful for the help..."

"Why do I feel that big but coming on?"

"But the last time we met with someone you recommended...?"

"Hey, I know, I know! But to be fair, I never said there was any guarantee. It's always proceed at your own risk. Move with caution. Ain't no different here. The guy says he thinks he may know something. All I'm doing is passing the info along to you. That's it. You want it? Great. I'll set it up. You don't? Fine. We can all move on. Up to you."

Recker didn't have to think it over for very long. Though skeptical, he wouldn't instantly turn down anything if there was even a slight possibility of it working out. They couldn't afford to pass things over without thoroughly checking them out. Bad leads, if it turned out to be that, were just part of the process.

"Yeah, OK. Set it up."

"How's now?" Tyrell asked.

"Now?"

"Yeah. You busy?"

"Uh, no, I guess not. Wasn't expecting it so soon, though. Especially in the middle of the day."

"I can make it later if you want."

"No, now's fine. Are you going to attend this meeting?"

"Well, like I said, I got a delivery." Tyrell could see by the look on his friend's face that he really wanted him to be there. "All right, fine, I can be there. You gotta give me an hour first. Gotta get some stuff loaded."

"Where are we meeting?"

"Let's make it Anthony's Pizza on 8th."

"A pizza shop?" Recker asked.

"I'm hungry."

"All right, that's fine. I'll meet you there. One hour. But you better not order ahead of time and put all that slop on there that you like."

Tyrell smiled. "Extra anchovies."

"If I smell that slop, I'm turning around and walking out."

Tyrell laughed and hung up. Recker turned to face his partners, both of whom were at the desk working. They could hear the conversation.

"What do you think?" Jones asked.

Recker shrugged. "All we can do is go there and listen. Whether we get anything out of it, that's a different story. We can hope."

Since it wouldn't take an hour to get to the pizza shop, Recker and Haley took their time in leaving. They still got there early, arriving approximately twenty minutes before the scheduled meeting. Recker took the liberty of ordering slices and a drink for everyone, so it was already waiting by the time Tyrell and his guest got there.

When Tyrell arrived, Recker noticed his friend stick his nose in the air. Tyrell glanced over at the table and shook his head as he approached.

"You did that deliberately."

"Did what?" Recker innocently asked.

"You deliberately got here ahead of time and ordered. That way you could be sure I got what you wanted."

"I did no such thing."

Tyrell and the other man sat down. He looked at the pizza, picked it up, and tossed it back down again.

"I mean, look at that. Plain. Who eats it plain?"

"I do," Recker answered.

"Yeah, because you're old and boring. That's what old, boring people do. Eat plain, boring food."

Recker slid the salt and garlic over to him. Tyrell swatted it away.

"Get out of here with that. That's not gonna disguise a dog."

Recker grinned. "It'll give it some flavor for you so it isn't plain."

"Yeah, OK." Tyrell looked at the pizza like he was agonizing over it. "I can't do this. I need some stuff on this thing."

He slid the piece over to the side. The other man quickly grabbed it.

"I'll take it. I ain't eat all day."

Tyrell got up. "I'll be right back. I gotta get me a real pizza."

Recker and Haley had already eaten theirs. Now, they were just sizing up the new guy sitting across from them.

"So you guys are them, huh?"

"We're what?" Recker said.

"You guys are The Silencers?"

Recker smiled. "That's the rumor."

"Man, it's good to meet you guys. Not that you really need an introduction or nothing, you know? Cause you guys are legendary out there."

"Nice to know we got a good reputation."

"So how long have you known Tyrell?" Haley asked.

"Must be going on ten years or so now. Long time. He's good people."

"Yeah, he is."

Tyrell then came back over to the table, with a new slice of pizza. This one had pepperoni and bacon on it. He pointed at it.

"See? Now that's what I'm talking about. Smothered with flavor. Now that's a pizza."

"At least it don't have anchovies on it," Recker said. "Cause I'd be walking out of here. I still don't know how you can eat that stuff."

"You just need to get an appreciation for it, that's all."

"No thanks."

Tyrell pointed with his thumb to the new guy. "Anyway, this is Trae."

"Look, I'll be straight with y'all," Trae said. "I got a record. I done some things. I've been in the joint for a year. I ain't no angel."

"Hard to find them these days," Recker replied.

"But when it comes right down to it, I'm not a bad

dude. I'm not in it for myself, pushing everyone else out of my way so I can make it to the top, you know what I mean?"

Recker nodded. "I get it."

"I'm just out there trying to make a living however I can. As long as nobody else gets hurt in the process. I know you guys will probably check me out or whatever, and I'm cool with that. I just wanted to be straight with you, let you know upfront."

"I appreciate that. Gets us off to a good start."

"How are your contacts?" Haley asked.

"My contacts are good. I mean, I wouldn't say I'm on Tyrell's level or anything. I mean, he was the goat. Still is. But I do all right for myself. He's up there in the major leagues and I'm in triple-a. Knocking on the door."

"You know something about these diamond robberies that have been going on?"

"Well, I've heard some talk about some things. Whether it's the same guys you're looking for, I can't say."

"What have you heard?" Recker asked.

"There's a lot of word about another place being hit next week. Nothing specific. But some talk about some big, shiny things going missing. Now, between you and me, that sounds like code for diamonds, you know?"

"Could be."

"So that's what made me think about those other

places that got hit lately. Started thinking maybe another job's coming up next week."

"What other info you got?"

"Right now? Nothing. Just that something might go down next week. If it's something you want me to put my head down on and run with it, I can try and find out more for you."

Recker stared at him for a moment, then his eyes went over to Tyrell. Tyrell nodded. That was good enough for Recker.

"OK. You dig around. See what you can find out. You better be discreet about it, though. I don't know who these guys are, so if they know you're onto them, I don't know if they'd hesitate to kill you. You need to know what you might be messing with."

"I'm good with risks," Trae said. "It don't bother me. And believe me, I ain't ready to meet my maker yet. So I ain't putting myself out there unnecessarily if I don't have to."

"Where'd you hear this rumor at? From who?"

"Just heard some guys talking, man. They were at the next table from me, talking about this stuff. I think they had a few too many, if you know what I mean. But I just sat there, listening. But they didn't say too much, other than those insinuations."

"How many people were there?"

"Three. Three of them. Just sitting around talking and drinking."

Recker glanced at his partner. Three of them. It

lined up with what they knew so far. At least they were off to a good start.

"You know their names or anything?" Recker asked.

"Nah. Never seen them before either. But I'm friendly with some of the people that work in the place we were in. So I can go back there and ask around without fear of anything. They can talk to me."

"OK. You do that. Let us know how it goes and all."

"Will do." Trae then started wiping his hands, looking like he was suddenly nervous. "Um, I almost hate to ask about this part."

"Yeah?"

"Like, I don't quite know how to say this, and I don't want you to think I'm greedy or something. But, um..."

"You're wondering about payment?" Recker said, knowing where this was going.

"Yeah. Like I said, I'm not like, greedy or something. And I don't even... I don't even have a number in mind or anything."

Recker could see the man was anxious about the subject and wanted to set his mind at ease.

"Don't worry about it. If the information is good, and you get more of it, you'll be taken care of."

"I can vouch for that," Tyrell said.

"I know you said that," Trae replied. "I just wanted to get it out in the open and all."

Recker was fine laying everything on the table ahead of time. It helped to reduce problems later on.

"If you have a constant stream of information we

can act on, whether it's just this, or whether it's other things and happening week after week, you'll get paid."

"And you'll be glad you did," Tyrell said.

"But it needs to be good. We don't pay for crap. And we don't put up with it either."

"Understood," Trae responded. "I get that. And I'm good with it. If I give you a bunch of nonsense, I don't deserve no money for it."

"We all whiff from time to time," Recker said. "But right off the bat? You need to prove you can step up to the plate and get a hit."

Trae nodded. "I hear ya. And I'll get on base for ya."

Recker then shook his hand. "We'll see."

8

Recker and Haley just got back from their trip to Boston. It was a little under six hours, but they were satisfied that the man they were seeing wasn't involved.

"Man, that guy was a total tool."

Recker snickered. "Yeah. But he seemed to be the most honest one we've come across. I don't think he was involved."

"Yeah, I'd agree. But man, I kind of wish he was. Kind of an arrogant prick that I'd be more than happy with knocking the smug smile off his face."

"I hear you. He did have a certain cockiness about him."

"A certain cockiness? That's putting it kindly."

"Well, you know me, I like to give people the benefit of the doubt."

They walked into the office, and were instantly

surprised to see that Jones wasn't there. They couldn't even remember the last time he wasn't in there.

"Did we step into a Twilight Zone episode?"

Recker double-checked the bathroom. "Maybe he just stepped out for a bit."

"He knew we were coming, right?"

"Yeah. I told him we were on the way."

They both immediately turned their heads toward the door when they heard it unlocking. Jones was a little surprised to see the both of them in there.

"What are you two doing here?"

"Uh, we work here," Recker answered. "Remember?"

"Yes, I've heard. I didn't realize you were coming back to the office, though." Jones looked at his watch. "It's after seven. I thought you'd both be going home."

"Well Mia's working, so I figured I'd just come here. Unless you prefer us not to be?"

Jones walked over to the desk. "Don't be silly. I just thought after the long drive you might be tired."

"Where were you just now?"

"Oh, I just took a walk. I sometimes do that during the evening when you two aren't around."

Recker and Haley glanced at each other. Recker was a little concerned for his friend.

"David, I know we've talked about this before, though not lately. But, don't you think it's time you put a little distance between you and the office?"

"A lot of work to be done," Jones replied.

"Most of it can wait. And you can automate a lot of it."

Jones got on the computer and started typing. He then stopped and rubbed his hands together. "One day."

"This operation won't work so well if you run yourself into the ground, you know?"

"I'm fine. That is why I take a daily walk."

"For what? Twenty minutes? Half hour?"

"It's enough. Besides, what else would you like me to do? This is what I've devoted my life to doing now."

"There's a difference between devoting your life to something and being fanatical about it."

"What else would you like me to do?"

Recker shrugged. "I don't know. Get an apartment again like you used to have. Take nights off. Come in late in the morning. Go to the theater, play chess, go antique shopping on the weekends. Have a hobby."

"Like you do?"

"Hey, you know I'm a baseball fan and watch games. I have the streaming package."

"Yes, I know."

"I'm just saying I think you need more of a work-life balance."

"Should I get married and have three kids while I'm at it?"

Recker rolled his eyes. "Let's not get ridiculous."

Jones smiled. "I get what you're saying. And you're right."

"I just don't want you to burn yourself out."

"Agreed. Once we have these diamond robbers under control, I'll look at slowing down."

"Until the next case comes along? We all know there'll be one."

"All I can say is I agree, and my intention is to do what you're suggesting."

"We'll help you get there," Haley said.

"I have no doubt of that."

Before they could come to any more of an agreement on the matter, they heard a phone ringing. It was coming from the desk drawer where Jones usually kept the spare phones. He opened the drawer and pulled out the one that was ringing. He looked at the unfamiliar number, curious as to who it was. He passed it over to Recker.

"I assume this is for you."

Recker shrugged. "Probably."

"Any ideas?"

"Guess I'll answer it and find out."

It was a number he passed out to several people over the past year. So no specific person jumped to the top of his mind. And the number that was calling was not familiar, though that wasn't exactly a surprise either. It made sense that if he had alternate numbers, the people he was dealing with had some too. In any case, he didn't waste time wondering, and eagerly answered.

"Well hello there," the voice said.

It was a familiar voice. One in which Recker had talked to recently. It took him a second or two to connect the voice to a face, but he did.

"Kavi Sharma," Recker said

"I was hoping you wouldn't forget me so soon."

"Not a chance."

"I suppose you're wondering about the nature of my call."

"Not really. I just figured you wanted to talk about the weather."

Sharma laughed. "A sense of humor. Always appreciated when you're dealing with an unpleasant profession."

"What's unpleasant?"

"You're the one asking about diamond robberies, are you not?"

"Are you calling because you have something to offer?"

"Perhaps I do," Sharma replied. "Do you have something to offer in return?"

"The thought of me busting down your door and ripping apart your entire business piece by piece isn't enough of an incentive to want to avoid it?"

Sharma slightly hesitated. "Uh, not so much. As much as you and your partner seem like a formidable duo, my security can be greatly enhanced from when we last saw each other."

"I'm sure of that."

"But I am not calling to butt heads. I am trying to offer an olive branch."

"For a price, I take it?"

"Everything has a price. Especially information."

"I'm not in the habit of buying it."

"I am not asking for a monetary contribution."

"Then what are you asking for?" Recker asked.

"Information in return."

"What do you think I have that would interest you?"

"For one, this is entirely a one-way conversation. You know quite a bit about me and I know absolutely nothing about you."

Recker didn't see the harm in letting him know that. Most other people did by now, anyway.

"They call me The Silencer."

"Ah, The Silencer. The famous vigilante from the big city. Your reputation travels far and wide."

"I wouldn't say New Jersey is far and wide. It's just over the bridge."

"Rumor has it that you're very tight with Vincent."

"I don't deal in rumors," Recker said, not really wanting to continue the conversation much longer if the man wasn't offering anything. "So do you have anything for me or not?"

"That would very much depend."

Recker was getting tired of feeling like they were playing a runaround game. "On?"

"I can use my extensive contacts to help you on this matter if you're willing to do me a favor."

"Which is?"

"I'd like for you to broker a meeting between Vincent and myself."

"Why?"

"I am trying to grow my empire, as small as it is."

"I haven't heard it's that small."

"Well, I suppose that's a relative term," Sharma said. "But Vincent controls Philadelphia and most of the surrounding areas."

"And that's a problem for you."

"Not so much of a problem as it is an opportunity."

"What, you wanna partner with him?"

"I feel there could be certain advantages for both of our organizations to join forces in certain avenues."

"Part of me feels like you should have the means to contact him yourself," Recker said. "What do you need a third party for?"

"Now we're getting into some complicated areas to which I really cannot say anything further. Let's just say those are my terms for helping you get all the information you require on these diamond robberies."

Recker was less than impressed with the offer, taking almost no time to think about it. "I'll pass."

Sharma was a little surprised the answer was no so quickly. "Perhaps you would like to take some time to think it over."

"I don't need time. Look, I don't know who you're

used to dealing with, but nobody uses me to help them further their criminal empire. I'm not a lackey that's going to pass messages back and forth and try to set up meetings between people I'm usually trying to stop and put out of business."

"Then I don't quite see what's in it for me."

"I already told you. Maybe by throwing me a bone, I won't decide to come put you out of business the next time I have a lull in my schedule."

Sharma chuckled. "Such boisterous and outlandish claims, if I may so so."

"You wouldn't be the first to think it. You can't ask the others, though. They're no longer around to verify it."

"Yes, I would imagine so. Such a shame. I was hoping we would be able to do some business."

"No, you were hoping to use me to further your business. And I'm not interested."

Recker didn't see the need to talk further, and hung up, tossing the phone back down on the desk.

"Sounds as though that didn't go so well," Jones said.

Recker huffed. "Guy want's a meeting with Vincent."

"Vincent? What for?"

Recker shrugged. "Who knows? Said he wants to partner with him for something."

Haley scoffed at the thought. "Yeah, right."

"You doubt that?" Jones asked.

"Yeah, I do. Look, guys like that can get word out to somebody through backchannels and whatnot. He don't need us to do that."

"Then why would he ask?"

"My gut feeling? He probably sees it as an opportunity to take out some competition and grow the easy way."

"You really think so? You think he would try to use us as an avenue to get closer to Vincent just to take him out?"

Haley pointed to the computer. "You got Sharma's information there. You see anything that makes you think he's not capable of that?"

Jones briefly glanced at his computer. "No."

"I'm not sure if that's his play," Recker said. "But I wouldn't say it's a far-fetched idea either. Sharma wants to expand, sees meeting with Vincent under the guise of a business meeting, wanting to partner up, only to actually set him up for an ambush? Plausible, I guess."

"But not likely?"

"I don't know how likely it is. I mean, it's not like he had days to think about this. He didn't even know who I was until five minutes ago. That's not much time to think about a play on Vincent."

"Unless he did know," Haley said. "There's cameras at the airport. Maybe even in his car, who knows? Maybe he did some digging and found out who we really were?"

Recker threw his hands up. "Anything's possible, I guess. But it doesn't really matter. I'm not interested in being anyone's gopher. We'll find out what we want on our terms. It may be the hard way... but it'll be our way."

9

Recker and Mia were out having dinner at a chain restaurant that they often liked visiting. With nothing new on the horizon regarding the diamond robberies, all they could do was wait on new information to fall into their laps. Without that, they could only carry on with their day.

"Let's go to a movie after this," Mia said.

"A movie? Why, what's playing?"

"Beats me. I don't even know. But we haven't been to a movie in such a long time. It's probably been well over a year."

"Yeah, it probably has."

"It doesn't even matter to me what it is. Romantic comedy, superhero, action, whatever. I'm good with anything."

Recker finished eating his cheeseburger. "Yeah, I guess if you want to, we can."

Mia had a huge smile on her face. "Great. We haven't had a real date night in a long time."

"What are you talking about? We go out to eat once a week."

"That's just dinner. A real date is like dinner and other things."

"Oh, is that the definition?"

"It is."

"Oh. I see. What is classified as other things?"

"You know. Like… things."

"Very illuminating. I wouldn't have guessed."

Mia laughed. "You know, we could go play pool, or maybe even go dancing. Things like that."

The look on Recker's face suggested he'd rather do anything other than those things.

"Dancing, huh? Pool?"

"That's what people do on dates."

Recker looked away from the table and puffed. Mia started laughing at him.

"Why does it look like you'd rather be subjected to a torture chamber than do any of those things?"

Recker smiled. "Well, it's not really that."

"Oh? Then what is it?"

"Well, it's… OK, it's really that."

"It's OK to do normal things."

Recker scrunched his nose. "Dancing isn't really my thing."

"I mean, you could just sit there in the corner and watch me dance with someone else."

"Uh, no."

"I'm just kidding. Not about the dancing part. Just about the someone else... you know what I mean."

Recker forced a smile. "I do."

"Would it really be so bad?"

Recker sighed and looked down. "Well, I guess it would depend on what kind of dancing you're talking about. Slow dancing? Maybe. If it involves any type of hip-wiggling, gyrating like a horny teenager, or making it seem like I'm looking for attention on the latest social media crazed app the world is raving out, I'm probably out."

"OK. How about we just figure out the next step after the movie?"

"I could probably live with that. Or, you know, we could just scrap everything after the movie and just go home."

"And do what?"

Recker grinned. "I've got something else in mind. Some other... activity."

"Oh. Do tell me more."

"You know, something that would make us both happy."

"I'm all ears."

Recker was just about to go further when his phone started to ring. Mia sighed and looked down and shook her head as Recker answered. The strange look on his face indicated it wasn't from one of his usual contacts.

"Trae?"

"Hey, man, just wanted to check in and let you know I got something for you."

"Oh yeah? What is it?"

"I got word that something's going down tonight."

"Tonight? What?"

"Word is that a jewelry store's getting hit."

"You know the details?" Recker asked.

"Rumor is that it's the one at the corner of 14th."

"How reliable do you think your sourcing is on this?"

"I think it's pretty good," Trae answered. "I heard it from a guy who says he was initially supposed to do the job, but he backed out at the last minute."

"Why?"

"Didn't really say. Think maybe he said it was too much risk or something. I'm not sure. Didn't really get to have a long conversation with the guy. Said it in passing."

"You know this guy?"

"Yeah, I mean, I seen him around a time or two. Not buds or hang out on the regular or nothing like that, but, yeah... seen him around."

"You got a specific time on this thing?" Recker asked.

"Word I got was that it was going down after closing."

"After closing? Or at closing?"

"Dude said after closing."

"Like when nobody else is there?"

"That's what he said."

"You think this is legit?"

"I mean, I can't say for sure," Trae replied. "I heard it, figured I'd pass it along to you. Could he just have had too much to drink and was spewing out nonsense? Maybe. Could he have had too much to drink and saying something he shouldn't have? Equally maybe. I don't really know. Like I said, I heard it, just wanted to pass it along to you. Maybe you'd wanna check it out."

"Did it seem like it had anything to do with those other diamond robberies?"

"Can't say. Nothing was mentioned about it. Don't really know. All I know is what I told you. That's it."

"All right. Thanks. I'll check on it."

"You got it. Let me know how it turns out, whether there's something to it or not. It'll help me to know whether to believe the guy again or not if I ever see him again."

"Yeah, I will. Thanks."

As soon as Recker put his phone away, he looked at Mia, who instantly knew what was going on. Nothing needed to be said.

"I take it you have to leave?"

"I'm sorry," Recker said. "I mean, I guess I could..."

"No, no, go ahead. Don't worry about me. I'll finish up here and pay the bill and all."

"I'll have Chris come pick me up so you can take the car home."

Recker sent Haley a message, letting him know what was going on, and telling him where he was.

"Is it the diamond stuff?" Mia asked.

"I don't know. Too soon to tell."

"I hope it is. That way it gets it out of the way."

"Me too."

"Then we can get back to normal. Imagine that. Me saying the rest of your job is normal."

Recker smiled and leaned over to kiss her cheek.

"I guess that ends date night," Mia said.

"I'm really sorry. I'll make it up to you."

"It's fine. Part of what I signed up for, right?"

"It shouldn't be, though."

"But it is. And I accept it."

"For now."

"For always," Mia replied.

Recker shook his head. "It won't be always. I promise you that."

"We'll see."

"Maybe if you want to wait up for me, we can still have that second part of our night that I was thinking about."

Mia's face lit up. "Oh? You mean that... mysterious activity?"

"I mean, only if you're up for it. If you're like, too tired or something..."

"Hush! I will be wide awake and waiting for you. Maybe in something... more appealing?"

Recker smiled. "Sounds like I can't wait to get back home."

Mia leaned over and kissed his lips. "Just make sure you don't rush too much and make a mistake."

"You know I won't."

10

Haley turned the headlights off as they got closer to the jewelry store. They were there before closing, so they parked along the street by a curb. There were other cars in front and in back of them. But they had a clear view of the front of the store, as well as an alley that went behind the building. So if someone showed up, they'd see them.

"How credible do you think this is?"

"No idea," Recker answered. "Guess we're about to find out, though."

"Sure would be nice if Trae is right on this. Would help us out on a lot of levels."

Recker agreed. "It'd give him a good step forward on how good his sources are. And if these are the people we're looking for."

"If these are the same people, they've changed their MO. The other three robberies were in the daytime."

"I know. It is over a week since the last one, so the timeline would match up. We'll just have to wait and see."

And they did wait. They mostly believed if a robbery happened, it would go down just as the store owner was locking up. It was a good time for most robberies. Fewer people around, the owner or manager would be counting money for the day, and there was an easier exit strategy with the lack of people.

But it didn't happen like that. At least not on this occasion. About an hour after the store closed, they saw the owner and another worker exit the store. Nothing seemed to be wrong. They continued watching as the two people got in their cars and drove away.

As more time passed, and there was nothing close to suspicious activity at the store, Recker and Haley were starting to believe they got this one wrong. Of course, Trae didn't give them a definitive word, and was just repeating what he'd heard, they really had hoped that he was right. Maybe they were just hoping he was right more than actually believing it.

Recker really wanted more ears on the street, and if Trae could provide that, they'd all be for the better because of it. He didn't have any illusions of someone taking Tyrell's place, at least not on the same level as Tyrell, Recker was still hoping to find someone reliable. Someone trustworthy. When they said something, Recker could take it to the bank. And while he was trying to keep his expectations in check here, he still held out hope. As the clock struck midnight, the two of them were starting to get restless.

"How much time you wanna give this?" Haley asked.

"A little more."

Recker thought of the girlfriend who was waiting at home for him, caught between wanting this scene to play out for a little while, and wanting to get home to be with her.

"Let's give it another hour or so. If nothing's happened by then, we'll pack it up and get out of here."

Another half hour passed before they got a hint of anything.

"Hey, hey, hey, what's that?" Haley said, pointing to the rear of the building.

Recker leaned forward, seeing a dark-colored van pulling in behind the store. Within a few seconds, it was no longer visible, completely concealed by the building. They remained in place for a few minutes, letting the team inside the van get to work before they confronted them.

An alarm was heard, but only for a brief second. It was then muted. Then they saw a light inside the store. It looked like it was from a flashlight.

"They got in there pretty quick," Haley said.

"Yeah, they did. Almost like they knew what they were doing."

"Almost. Silenced an alarm, and got inside, in what... just a couple minutes?"

"All right, let's move in," Recker said.

Haley started the car and put it in drive, getting to the store in no time. He pulled in behind the building, in the same direction the van had gone. They saw and pulled in behind it. Recker and Haley jumped out of the car, but they didn't go very far.

Almost immediately, a member of the crew jumped out of the back of the van and started shooting at them. He was concentrating on Recker, so Haley leaned around the driver's side door and pumped a couple rounds into him. There was another man at the back of the door to the jewelry store. Once he saw what was going on, he jumped into the action, as well. He took aim at Haley, one of the bullets going through the window of their SUV, causing Haley to duck behind the door.

Recker moved around to the hood, giving himself a good line of sight to the man. He pulled the trigger three times, dropping the man in an instant. Three more men ran over to the door from inside the store.

"What's going on out there?!" one of them shouted. "Joey, you good?! Robbie?!"

"Your friends are gone," Recker replied. "Throw your guns out and give it up."

Recker didn't get the reply he was hoping for. Instead of a confirmation, and a bunch of guns being tossed out the door, he got a few bullets in return.

None of them landed, though a few of them did lodge into the car. He looked at some of the damage to the vehicle and shook his head.

"We're gonna have to get some bulletproof metal or something."

Haley briefly returned fire, keeping the men inside the store. They knew something was going to have to give, though. At some point, the police would arrive. Or the men would try to make a break for it, not wanting to get caught up in that building with no escape, and completely surrounded.

Recker took a few steps back to the passenger door so he could speak to his partner more easily.

"Chris, maybe you should head around to the front."

"Think they might make a break for it out there?"

"If they see back here's covered, and they take a look out there and see nothing, what would you do?"

"Go out the front," Haley replied. "I'll head over."

"Just be careful."

Haley quickly bolted from his position, running to the side of the building. He was at an angle in which he didn't think he was in much danger of being hit if there was gunfire. Luckily, there wasn't even an attempt to gun him down as he left the car.

He quickly ran around to the front of the building, getting there just in time to see the door open. One man bolted from the store. Considering there was no car in the vicinity, the man had no destination in mind.

He just appeared to be trying to get as far away from the scene as he possibly could.

"Hey!" Haley yelled.

The man instantly turned around, brandishing an automatic rifle in hand. He pointed it in Haley's direction and got a few rounds off. Haley dropped to the pavement as the bullets flew over his head. He then unleashed several rounds from his pistol. The man went down. Haley couldn't be sure whether the man was dead, but he didn't appear to be moving.

Haley kept his eyes on the door in case any of the man's buddies also tried to exit. Nobody seemed anxious to follow in the other man's footsteps, though.

"We give up!"

Haley heard the voices coming from the back of the building. He quickly ran back around there, stopping at the edge of the building. He peeked his head around and saw two men walking out the back door, holding their hands up high. Recker was moving around the front of the car to cover them better. Haley also emerged from his position.

"How'd you guys get here so fast?" one of the men asked.

Neither Recker nor Haley responded.

"Grab the ties," Recker said.

Haley went to the trunk of their car where they kept some supplies in case they needed them in times such as these. He removed some zip ties and brought them over to the group. He brought the hands of both men behind their backs and tied their hands together.

"You wanna take pictures?" Recker asked.

"Yeah."

Haley got out his phone and started with the two men alive and breathing. Once he was done with them, he started with the dead men. Recker led the other two men over to their van. He opened the back door and sat them both down.

"Did you guys pull off those other robberies?" Recker asked.

"What other robberies?"

Recker relayed the places, dates, and times from memory. "Any of those ring a bell?"

"Nope."

Recker couldn't tell if the man was being honest, or just defiant. Sometimes the two were in close proximity to each other. As Haley came back around after taking the picture of the man out front, they could hear police sirens. They were getting closer.

"Lay down," Recker said.

"What?!"

"I said lay down."

Recker pushed the man onto their backs. Then Haley went over to them and tied their feet together. With the police on the way, and getting closer with each second, Recker and Haley couldn't stick around any longer. But they also didn't want their new friends to walk away after they left. Now, they were pretty much stuck. They pushed the men further inside the van, then closed the door.

"Just sit tight," Recker said. "We'll get you out in a bit."

Recker and Haley quickly jogged back to their car and jumped in. They pulled around the van and went down the other side of the alley, knowing the police were probably coming in the same way everyone else had.

Just as they got to the other end of the alley, they could see the police lights flashing in the rearview and side mirrors. They escaped just in the nick of time.

"Got a little close on that one," Haley said.

Recker continued looking in the mirrors as they drove down the street. "Yeah."

They even passed a police car coming in the opposite direction, probably going towards the jewelry store. Since they weren't driving fast, or erratically, there was nothing to suspect that the car they were in was in any way involved with what happened. They passed the patrol car without incident.

"Head back to the office and figure this out?"

Recker thought about it for a second. "No. Let's wait until tomorrow. If this was them, it's taken care of. And waiting won't make any difference."

"And if it's not?"

"Then these guys aren't likely connected to the group we're looking for, anyway. So it still won't make any difference."

"Yeah, probably right."

"Besides, I have... Mia's been waiting for me to get home."

Haley smiled. "Oh. Should I tell David you might be coming in late tomorrow?"

Recker laughed, though he wasn't ready to commit to anything. "We'll see."

"Well if you're still not in by nine, I won't send the Coast Guard out looking for you."

Recker smirked. "Sounds good."

"I'll drop you back off. What's your gut say on these guys we just took out?"

"I don't know. Something's telling me they're not the ones we're looking for."

"We didn't give them a chance to grab anything, so we don't know if they were just going for diamonds or everything they could get their hands on."

"Even more than that, like you said, their MO was different. Late at night. Five guys instead of three."

"My gut's telling me we still got work to do. This ain't them. Hope I'm wrong, but... I dunno."

Recker nodded, tending to agree with his partner. "Yeah. Still got work to do."

11

By the time Recker showed up the following morning, it was after ten o'clock. When he stepped foot in the office, his friends greeted him like they hadn't seen him in months.

"There he is!" Haley said.

Recker seemed embarrassed by the attention. "I'm only a couple hours later than usual."

"You know, you look refreshed, but tired, at the same time."

Recker smiled. "Yeah. Funny how that goes."

"We won't ask about why you're late," Jones said. "Since it's already a given."

"All right, all right, everyone's had their fun. Let's get on with the day's events."

"Well, while you were..." Jones cleared his throat. "Anyway, thanks to the pictures you guys took last night, I was able to run down everyone involved in the robbery."

"And?"

Jones pointed to the big TV on the wall, putting the information, and the headshots of the men involved, on the screen. Recker walked over to the screens and stood in front of them, reading the information. Three men died, and two were captured.

"All career criminals," Recker said.

"The license plate on the van also comes back as stolen," Jones said.

Haley went over to the screen and pointed at the picture on the far left. "This guy's probably the ringleader. One of the guys we tied up."

Recker nodded as he looked at the picture. "Suspected of several other robberies."

"Every single one of them has experience in this type of thing."

Recker was looking at the five men on the screen, while also thinking about the three diamond robberies that already happened, trying to connect the dots between the two.

"What are you thinking?" Jones asked.

Recker shook his head, not even sure himself. "I don't know. I'm just not feeling it. It doesn't feel like the same crew."

"I was able to get my hands on some police information. They had already started stuffing a duffel bag with valuables. Diamonds, to be precise."

Recker snapped his head around to look at him. "Diamonds? That's it?"

"That's all they had in the bag by the time you rolled up on them."

"We didn't give them much time to collect anything else."

"Perhaps not. They only had a few diamonds in there. But... that was all they had."

Recker turned back to the screen, rubbing his face, then underneath his chin.

"What is it specifically that's bothering you?" Jones asked.

"A few things. One, these guys are all experienced. We were going with the theory that we were looking for people that were not as experienced. That's why they were working jobs that were upping in value."

"That was our working theory. It didn't mean it was correct. Or set in stone."

"There's also five guys here. Only three on the others."

While Jones didn't have an answer for that, Haley did.

"Might still fit," Haley said. "Only three guys went into the store last night. One was in the van. The other was outside as a lookout. So they might have had a similar setup in the other places. Maybe both were in the getaway car. Or one was near the front door in all three spots."

Recker wasn't sure he bought that, but couldn't dismiss it either. "Maybe."

"This was also at night. The others were earlier in the day."

"Could be they're getting worried about being predictable. Having a pattern. Just want to change it up. It'd be smart to do that."

"Yeah, it would." Recker turned back to Jones. "What about these other robberies these guys are suspected of? None of the three we're checking?"

Jones reached for a piece of paper on the desk, then handed it over to his partner. "No, all completely unrelated. There's a list of five on there, though."

Recker eagerly read the list. "Not all of these are jewelry stores. Not all diamonds, either."

"Doesn't necessarily mean anything in and of itself. He might have found something that he thought works. Why change it up?"

Recker grimaced as he lowered his head and scratched the back of his head. "Seems like we're trying to justify a lot of reasons as to why they still might be the guys."

"As you're doing in trying to justify that they aren't."

"I guess that's fair." Recker's phone rang, and he answered it. "Yeah?"

"Hey, just wanted to see how that information panned out last night?" Trae asked.

"Turned out to be good. There was an attempted robbery at the jewelry store. Right around midnight."

"Sweet. I take it you were able to stop that?"

"Yeah, we took care of it."

"Nice. Glad it turned out OK. Um, listen, about the payment arrangement and all... um, not that I'm like in a hurry or anything, or bugging or nothing, but..."

"Don't worry about it," Recker said. "Just text me how you want it. ACH, Venmo, PayPal, whatever you want. I'll make sure you're taken care of."

"That's great, man. Thanks. I don't want you to think I'm pressing or anything, I'm just... I really need the money and all. But no rush or anything."

"What's your living situation right now?"

Trae cleared his throat. "Um, you know, just, uh, I got a place. It's just me. Nobody else. It's a small place over some dry cleaning store. Rent's not too bad and all."

"You like it there?"

"Yeah, you know, it's not too bad. I mean, it's all right, I guess. Just a one bedroom, one bath type of thing. Not very big, but since it's just me, it works out all right. Maybe one day I'll get one of those big skyscraper places over by Rittenhouse or something, you know?"

"What about family?" Recker asked.

"Nah, it's pretty much just me. My parents kicked the bucket a while back, and my older brother died from a drug overdose a couple years ago. I got a younger sister, but I don't see too much of her. She went to college down in Tennessee. Then she met some guy there, and they got married, then stayed there. So I think they're looking to start a family soon. I mean, I talk to her every now and then, but I haven't seen her in a year or so. And I ain't got no wife or girlfriend or nothing at the moment, so... it's basically just me."

"Sometimes works out better that way."

"Yeah, I ain't complaining. Got no commitments, nothing holding me down, telling me what to do, it's all good."

Recker sensed an opportunity to help develop Trae into what they had lost with Tyrell slowing down.

"So you wanna keep working on this?"

"Yeah, whatever you need," Trae answered. "I'm down with whatever."

"Keep your eyes and ears open at all times. Work whatever sources you have. Cultivate new ones. If you wanna work for me full time, I want you knowing this city, and everyone in it, like the back of your hand. I don't want anything happening that you don't know about."

"I can do that."

"But that means not charging ahead like a bull in a china shop. You gotta work in the shadows. People can't know who you are or your connection to me. Once they know that, things can get messy. Maybe sources dry up. Plus, it puts you in danger if people think they can use you to get to me."

"I'm down with that."

"It also means it could get dangerous at times. Can't guarantee your life won't get threatened at some point."

"Hey, I came up on the streets, man. Danger isn't a foreign concept for me."

"What about transportation?" Recker asked. "How do you get around?"

"Uh, usually just walk. Or I'll take a bus or something. Hitch a ride if I need to."

"You got a license?"

"Driver's license? Yeah, I got one. Still valid. I ain't got no car, though."

"I'll take care of that. I want you to be able to move around quickly. Waiting around for bus times don't work for me."

"You're gonna get me a car?!"

"It's not gonna be Benz or anything," Recker said. "I don't want you sticking out like a sore thumb. It'll be used, but in good condition."

"I can't really pay you for that."

"Consider it part of the job. If you're working for me, I expect you to work it out there. You need to know things."

"I won't let you down. I promise you that."

"There's one more thing. Anyone that works with me, I expect their unmatched and undivided loyalty. That goes both ways. If you're trustworthy, and do everything that's expected, you can always count on me. No matter what. And I mean that. Whatever the situation, personal, financial, work-related, I will always be there."

"I appreciate that."

"But if I ever feel that trust is not earned, or you turn on me, there is no place on this earth that you'll be able to hide."

"I feel you on that, man. I promise you, that's nothing you'll ever have to worry about with me. I won't ever turn on a friend or a partner, you know? I'm one of those captains that goes down with the ship, you feel me?"

"Yeah, I feel you. Back to business, though, I need you right now to keep your ears open about those diamond robbers. I'm not sure the guys we got last night were the same ones."

"I'll start poking around. For sure."

"Remember. In the shadows. You're no good to anyone if you're dead. Especially yourself."

"No worries. People won't even know I'm there."

"OK. Send me your info and I'll get you set up."

"Right on."

After Recker hung up, he could feel the stares of his partners.

"Bringing him into the fold already?" Jones asked. "A little quick, don't you think?"

"He was right on the money."

"This time. But it was only one time. Why not work him in slowly? Let him prove himself over the course of weeks or months before bringing him in full time?"

Recker shrugged. "I don't know. I guess it's just a gut feeling."

Jones looked at their other partner.

"I got a good feeling about him too," Haley replied.

"Look, if it doesn't work, we can rectify it," Recker said. "But by bringing him in now, we can help mold him into what Tyrell was. Give him a bigger meaning. Give him a role. Let him see how things can be if he puts in the work."

"And a car?"

"A ten or fifteen thousand dollar car. Used. No big deal. Money's not our concern, right?"

"This is true."

"And if he can even get close to Tyrell's level, it'll be money well spent. And he'll have earned it."

"I'll get to work on it," Jones said.

Recker turned back to the screen on the wall, looking at the pictures of the five men. In his heart, he didn't believe these were the same men they were looking for. He couldn't guarantee it, but something inside was tugging at him that the men they were after were still out there. Just waiting to strike again.

12

———

Three more days went by, and the team was no closer to finding out the truth about the diamond robbers than before. On one hand, it was good that nothing appeared to be on the horizon, and while some might assume that was because the suspects had already been killed and apprehended, Recker didn't share those beliefs. He still thought the threat was out there.

But if that was the case, they hadn't made any progress. Part of their attention had been diverted elsewhere, as other things popped up that they had to work on. But every time they came back to it, nothing new appeared. Trae hadn't heard anything, and Jones hadn't come up with anything different. They were at a standstill for the moment.

Recker was sitting in the booth at Vincent's favorite diner. He was earlier than usual for these meetings.

Usually Vincent was already there and waiting. This time, Recker had already been there for half an hour. And while they sometimes shared intel about things either of them were working on, that wasn't the basis for this meeting. No, for this, Recker had something else on his mind.

As Vincent walked in, Malloy, and other guards surrounding him, they walked down to the table. The guards slowly drifted away like they normally did. Only Malloy escorted him when Vincent finally sat down. Recker and Malloy gave each other a nod to greet each other, then Malloy took up his usual position, watching for any signs of trouble.

Vincent chuckled as he looked down at the empty table and pointed at it. "You couldn't have anything waiting for me?"

Recker grinned. "Wasn't sure what you were in the mood for."

Vincent patted his stomach. "Just as well. I'm watching what I eat for the next few weeks. Put on a few pounds lately."

"Aren't we all?"

"So, what's this about? Need help on something?"

Recker shook his head. "No, this isn't really about me. This is about you."

"Oh? Did I step on somebody's toes recently?"

"I guess that would depend. What do you know about a man named Kavi Sharma? You know him?"

The way Vincent's face contorted indicated he was

surprised to hear the name. "Kavi Sharma? Yes, I know him. Well, I know of him."

"Not a regular business partner?"

"Not any business partner. Why do you ask about him?"

"I've had a couple meetings with him," Recker answered.

"Oh. Mind if I inquire about the nature of these meetings?"

"Nothing to do with you. There's some diamond heists that have happened recently. His name came up as someone worth looking into."

"Ah, yes, I'm assuming you're talking about those... what was it? Three robberies?"

"Those are the ones. In five weeks."

"Yes, I've heard about those. I'm afraid I don't have any inside information for you about that."

"Didn't think you would. I'm not here about that, anyway. I can handle that. I'm mostly here to talk to you about Sharma."

"What's there to talk about?"

"It could be nothing," Recker said. "Or maybe I'm just overly cautious. Or maybe I'm just thinking of things that aren't really there. But I get the sense that he's gunning for you."

"Gunning for me? Why?"

"Well, after I told him who I was, he talked about rumors of you and I working together at times."

Vincent put his hand up. "Say no more. Let me

guess. He wanted you to initiate a meeting between him and I."

"That's right."

Vincent laughed. "That guy has been trying to get my attention for almost two years now."

"So you haven't met him?"

"No. I'm not interested."

"I thought maybe he was trying to take you out or something."

"An interesting thought."

"What's he want?"

"He wants what everybody wants. Power. Power is a dangerous drug when it's in the hands of the wrong person."

"Doesn't he already have it?" Recker asked.

"In New Jersey, sure. But he wants more."

"And that's where you come in?"

Vincent nodded. "That's where I come in. He's hoping to join forces with me. Some kind of merger with our organizations. At least that's what I hear from my sources. I haven't met with the man directly... because I'm not interested. He's made overtures in that regard, hoping it'll get back to me. He's desperate for it to happen."

"But why? He's already got his own territory, doesn't he?"

"He's small time. His organization's only a tiny fraction of mine. He's hoping that by joining our groups together, his stature will only increase significantly. But

I'm not in the business of letting others ride on my coattails."

"So you don't think he's after you or something?"

"No, I don't think so. At least, not at this time. Now, maybe that's his ultimate goal. Get in so deep with me that he'll eventually have the means, money, and power to overthrow me or assassinate me or something. But I don't believe that is his goal at the moment."

"Why would he think you'd even be interested?" Recker asked.

"I won't deny that his organization shows some promise, and rumor has it that he's got a stranglehold on the territory that he has, it's still a small territory. He's looking to branch out."

"Using you as a means to do that?"

"That's what I assume."

"From what you know of him, do you think he could be involved in those diamond robberies? From my conversation with him, I didn't think he was, but maybe you know something I don't."

Vincent leaned his elbow on the table and put his hand on his chin as he thought about it. "I would tend to think not. Those robberies weren't big-time scores, were they? I mean, in the grand scheme of things."

"About a hundred thousand total," Recker replied.

"Yeah, I don't think that would pique Sharma's interest. I could be wrong. I don't know the man well. But everything I've heard about him is that he's a bigger risk taker. These robberies don't sound like they fit the bill. A million dollars, sure, maybe. But for a hundred thousand? In three tries? I tend to doubt it."

"That's what I figured too. But he was willing to help me out with it if I could facilitate a meeting between you."

"Should I clear a spot out in my calendar?"

"No, I told him I wasn't interested in being a matchmaker."

"Since the robberies happened here, it's quite likely he has no idea what's going on anyway. And I doubt he could find out. He doesn't have the contacts."

"He was mentioned as a person of interest."

"Oh, I have no doubt of that," Vincent said. "On a bigger score, if someone wanted to unload them, I believe he'd be able to get rid of them. And it's equally as possible on a bigger score that he might even be behind it. But on a smaller scale, in which he's not involved, I don't believe he could offer you much. Especially when it wasn't done on his turf. He's a player, but not if he's not directly involved. And if you don't believe he is, all he can do is suck you down a tube going nowhere. He's only interested in growing his stature."

"Good to know. Thanks."

"I can, of course, keep my ears out in case I hear anything. I'll pass it along to you if I do."

"I'd appreciate that."

"As far as Sharma goes, my advice would be to

ignore him for the foreseeable future. Unless you've got your own business with him. But other than that, he's got nothing to offer you. I would stay clear."

After Recker and Vincent wrapped up their meeting, Recker stopped for a few minutes to talk to Malloy. Once that was done, he walked out of the diner. On the way back to the car, he heard his phone ringing. When he saw that it was Trae, he eagerly answered, hoping his new go-to man would have something for him. He wasn't disappointed.

"Hey, I just wanted to tell you about this real quick," Trae said in a hurried tone. "Something's going down."

"Something's going down? Like what?"

"Like those diamond robberies. Man, it is all over the street that it's about to happen."

"Another robbery? When?"

"Today! It's like... I'm hearing it all over. I've heard it from like six different sources. They're all telling me they got word that another heist is going down."

"When and where?"

"I got conflicting reports on that. I got the place. Not sure about the time, though."

"What have you heard?" Recker asked.

"Monty's Jewelry. Over on 52nd. A couple people said it's gonna be in three hours. And a couple people said it's happening... right about now."

"Now?!"

"That's the word I'm getting. I can't confirm either time yet."

"You think it's legit?"

"Six people gave me the name. Seems pretty legit to me. It's just the time nobody can agree on."

"All right, thanks. I'm on it."

"Good luck."

Recker immediately placed a call to his partner. "Chris, I just got word from Trae, looks like there's another robbery going down."

"What time?"

"It's either now or in three hours. Couldn't pin a time down."

"Heading over there now?"

"Yeah, why don't you meet me there?" Recker said. "Monty's Jewelry on 52nd."

"He's pretty sure about this?"

"Said he heard it from six different people."

"Seems as legit as it gets."

"Yeah, we'll see."

"I'll be there," Haley said. "Leaving now."

"I'll see you there." Recker rushed over to his car and jumped in. "Hopefully this is it."

13

Recker was already closer to Monty's Jewelry than Haley was, so he got there first by about five minutes. He first drove by the store, taking a good hard look through the store window. He saw someone behind the counter, though it looked like an employee. There also appeared to be a couple other people in the store, though considering nobody had hoods on, they looked like they were customers.

As Recker continued driving, he spun his head around, looking for a car nearby that would've held the suspects in it. He didn't initially see anything that was suspicious. He was looking for a car that was just parked along the side of the road with three men in it, just sitting there doing nothing. Or maybe they'd be looking around like he was. He saw no signs of anyone that fit the bill, though.

Recker drove completely around the block, still

looking for what he assumed was three men, though the exact number wasn't really what he was focused on. If there were two or four, that wouldn't have been surprising either. But after he came back around to the front of the building, he still saw no signs of any potential problems.

Instead of driving around for a while, Recker pulled over to the side of the road, parking in between two other cars. He was no longer directly in front of the jewelry store, as now he was further down the street. But he could see the front door to the building clear as day. A few minutes later, his phone went off.

"Hey, I'm here," Haley said. "Did I miss the festivities?"

"Haven't missed anything yet."

"No-show?"

"So far."

"Trae said he couldn't pin a time down, right?"

"That's what he said," Recker replied.

"Got a gut feeling?"

Recker stared at the store for a bit, then looked at scores of people walking up and down the sidewalk on both sides of the street. It looked like any other ordinary day. It sure didn't have the feeling of trouble about the hit. That was the thing about trouble, though. It sometimes came out of nowhere.

Recker let out a sigh. "I don't know. I don't really have a feeling on this one. Maybe it's it. Maybe it's not."

"Where are you at? I'll set up in the opposite direction."

"South end. Past the intersection. I'm on the same side as the store."

"OK. I'll park up on the north side on the opposite side of the store. We should be able to choke them off if they come by."

While they waited, they started discussing different strategies in the event that they had to jump into action. Of course, most of it would be dictated by what the robbers did. If they had someone outside watching, Recker and Haley wouldn't be able to sneak up on anyone. If there was no one waiting in the car, and no one watching the door, Recker could put a tracker on the car in case they lost them. Or they could go inside like gangbusters and take everyone out.

As Recker surveyed the area, though, he didn't quite like what he was seeing. They were in the middle of the day. There was a lot of activity on the sidewalks. If something happened, and they rushed in there and started shooting, a few wild shoots could end the life of an innocent bystander. That was obviously not something Recker wanted. They'd have to be careful.

After a few more minutes went by, they were starting to think they had a dud. At least at this point of time. Maybe the deal would go down later. But it didn't seem to be happening now.

"It's looking like we're gonna have a longer wait," Haley said.

Recker wasn't ready to give up on it quite yet. "Maybe."

He knew things like this were never exact. Especially when they were dealing with third-party information. Sometimes others weren't on the same timeline as they were. Waiting was just part of the deal. Then, Recker noticed a white car pulling up in front of the store. It was driving slow, which is what drew his attention to begin with. The car then parked by the curb.

"Chris, you see a white car just pull up in front?"

"Yeah, can't quite see who's in there, though."

"Me neither. Keep your eyes open."

They didn't have to wonder for long. Three doors immediately opened up, with three men getting out. Curiously, the only door that didn't open was the one to the driver's side. Three men started walking towards the store. They all had long coats on, which was an instant giveaway. It wasn't that cold out.

"This might be it."

"Wanna go in?" Haley asked.

"I didn't see a driver get out."

"We can take him out on the way in."

Recker's eyes darted to both sides of the street. He saw a woman pushing a stroller on the side of the jewelry store. He saw an elderly couple on the other side, moving slowly, the wife helping her husband move around. He looked in his side mirror, seeing a group of four or five kids, probably eighteen or nineteen, holding basketballs, on their way to a court. There were also a few cars driving by.

"Mike?"

By now, Recker looked back at the store again, just in time to see the three men putting black ski masks on and entering the store. There was no question now that this was it.

"We can get them on the way out too."

Recker was still glancing around, seeing all the potential downfalls to engaging the group. He couldn't say any of the risks were worth it.

"There's too many people around."

"Not if we barge in there," Haley said.

"If we take out the driver on the way in, they'll hear it and be ready by the time we get there. It doesn't give us the advantage."

As Recker continued looking around, the amount of people on the street didn't lessen. If anything, even more people appeared. He wasn't going to chance it. But he did have other ideas on how to approach this.

"Let's let them go through with this," Recker said. "But we can still tail them until we get to a better location."

"How you wanna work it?"

"I'll drive past them. I'll grab a picture of their plate and send it to David. That way if we lose it, hopefully he'll be able to pick them up on a camera somewhere."

"What if we hear gunshots?"

"Then all bets are off."

Haley was on board with the plan. Recker pulled out of his spot and started driving down the street. As he drove toward the store, he got a clear view of the license plate of the white car. He even took a pic of the driver as he passed him. The man was mostly looking toward the jewelry store, so Recker didn't get a great shot of him. But maybe they could do something with it in the event they lost him.

Once he got further down the street, Recker pulled over to the side of the road again. He would wait there until the white car went past him, then he'd start his tail. If for some reason, the car reversed and went in the other direction, then Haley would start the first leg of the tail. In either case, no matter where it went, Recker and Haley would take turns in being the lead vehicle. It was a common strategy when multiple cars were involved, and helped to avoid being spotted. Instead of someone looking back and seeing the same car behind them constantly, they'd see different vehicles, and hopefully they weren't observant enough to recognize that they were switching off.

They knew they wouldn't have to wait long. And they didn't. But while they were, Recker sent a picture of the license plate to Jones. The robbers then came charging out of the store after only a few minutes. They jumped into the car, which instantly took off, barreling down the street.

"Here we go," Haley said. "Coming your way."

Recker saw the car coming in his side mirror. Once

they drove past him, he started to pull out. Haley pulled out of his spot, as well, though he started driving in a different direction, hoping to meet up with them in a few more minutes.

It seemed like a clean job. There didn't seem to be any commotion coming from the store's direction. They couldn't hear any yelling or screaming, nobody running in any direction, no sirens, nothing.

The white car was driving fast, wanting to put as much distance between them and the store as they could, so Recker had to put a little more speed in the pedal than he liked. But he still couldn't make it seem like he was hot on their heels and following them. He still had to keep some distance between them, as hard as that might seem.

Recker let the white car get some separation as he fell back a little. He still had the car in his sights, but he couldn't get into a race with them. If there were no other alternatives he would, but high-speed chases on the road usually didn't turn out so well. And he wasn't going to put anyone else on the road in danger.

After a few more minutes on the road, the white car finally started slowing down. They were obeying traffic signals, and going the speed limit. Now that they were further away from the jewelry store, and there were no police cars in sight, or sirens heard, they didn't have to be in as much of a hurry. Now it was time to just act like they were anybody else on the road.

Recker and Haley were communicating the whole

time. And once Recker saw Haley in his mirror, Recker turned off the road, letting his partner take up the tail. Recker would continue driving in a parallel direction for when it was his time to be the lead car in the pursuit again.

"I'll give you about five minutes, then I'll come in again," Recker said.

"Roger that. Wish I could figure out where they're going."

"Maybe they have a corporate headquarters."

Haley laughed. "Yeah, maybe. Heading for the board of directors meeting."

"They either have a designated spot where they split everything up, or maybe a spot where they're stashing everything."

"Could be a public storage place."

"Yeah, could be. Doesn't really matter where it is, though. Wherever it is, we're gonna be there."

14

Recker and Haley continued switching off, doing their usual excellent job in remaining undetected as they pursued the robbers. Jones caught the white car on several cameras, so even if Recker and Haley had lost them, they wouldn't have gotten too far away. Luckily, Jones wasn't even needed so far.

Recker and Haley had just switched spots again, with Recker only a few cars behind the white vehicle now. They were on the edge of the city, and it looked like they were about to go into one of the suburbs.

"How far you think these guys are going?" Haley asked.

"I dunno. Kind of surprised it's lasted this long, to be honest."

"You don't think they spotted one of us, do you?"

"No, I don't think so. I think if they had, they'd be

showing us a lot of smoke. They wouldn't be driving like Miss Daisy right now."

"Good point."

"No, they got somewhere to be. Just haven't gotten there yet."

Thankfully, it didn't take that much longer. The car traveled into Lower Merion Township, which was a part of Montgomery County, and part of the Philadelphia Main Line. They drove for another ten minutes before they finally arrived at what appeared to be the destination.

Recker pulled over to the side of the road as he waited for his partner to get there. Haley got there within five minutes. Recker still had sight of the men as they got out of their vehicle and walked inside the building. Haley's car pulled up behind that of his partner's. He got out of his car and hopped in the passenger seat of Recker's car.

"What do we got?" Haley asked.

"All four are still in that building. All got out, grabbed a bag, which I assume was whatever they took from that jewelry store, and jogged inside. Still in there."

"What's the play?"

Recker took a look around. The building was off the main road, and surrounded by trees. There didn't appear to be any other traffic around, either on foot or by car. It was a pretty isolated spot. Seemed perfect for what this group was doing.

"I think if we split up, go in on different sides, we should be able to flush them out."

Haley nodded as he surveyed the area as well. "Sounds like a plan."

"I wanna take out a couple of those tires first. Just in case one or two try to escape, they won't have anywhere to go. Unless it's on foot."

Haley took a look at the position of the car. It wasn't directly in front of the building, but off to the side a little.

"I can do that." He took out a small pocket knife. "I can do a little slashing as I make my way to the back. It's right on the way."

"OK. As soon as you disappear around the building, I'll start making my entry."

"How do you wanna do this? Take them out? Capture them? Sweat them for answers?"

"I think that's gonna depend on them and how they wanna play it. We can give them the chance to surrender. But if they come up shooting instead... let them have it."

Recker and Haley got out of the car, gently closing the door so as to not make a sound with it. With their guns out, they walked over to the front group of trees that led into the round parking area. Haley took a peek around the tree to make sure there was no guard stationed or that no one was looking at them. With the coast seemingly clear, he took off running for the white car, keeping his body as low to the ground as possible.

He safely made it to the car. He then punctured several large holes in the rear tire on the passenger side. Haley then crawled toward the front of the car and gashed a few more rips in that one too. The air immediately started filtering out of the tires and the car shifted. That car was going nowhere in a hurry. He took a look back at his partner and nodded, letting him know the job was done if he couldn't see it himself.

Haley took a quick look over the hood at the building, then ran full speed towards the side of it. There was a window there, but Haley ducked underneath it, as he made his way around to the back. Recker then immersed himself within the trees to hide his movements. There was a wide open space directly in front of the building, so at some point, he was going to have to make himself vulnerable. Unless he came up on the building from the side, and slid his way over. That seemed to be the best strategy, rather than making himself a wide open target.

Recker maneuvered through the trees until he got to the other side of the building, then made a quick run to it. There was no window on that side of the building, so there was no danger of someone taking a potshot at him. Before he was able to move any further, he heard a familiar and distinctive sound. The popping sounds of gunfire that he'd heard all too often over the years.

He knew what that meant. Haley had already found the men. Or they found him. Regardless, he was already engaged. That meant that the odds of finding a peaceful resolution to this situation was pretty much guaranteed to be non-existent.

Recker peeked around the corner, having a feeling that if there was conflict around the back, that usually meant someone was going to be going in the opposite direction. That was usually the way it went. Unless they were going up against a group of stone-cold killers, there was always a person or two who didn't have the stomach to stand and fight. Or they were too worried about being caught and just wanted to get away as fast as possible, leaving everyone else behind.

Recker wasn't going to stand there and wait too long, though. If his partner was already in trouble and engaged, he wasn't going to leave Haley hanging out to dry like that. Especially since Recker already knew how many people were inside.

Luckily, he didn't have to wait long. That was the good part about having as much experience as he did. He'd seen all these situations before. And most of them played out in similar fashions. This was no different.

The front door opened, and a man immediately came running out. He was heading for the car. From Recker's vantage point, it looked like the driver of the car. He recognized the hair color and style as he drove past the car in front of the store.

"Hey!" Recker shouted.

He just wanted to get the man's attention. The man

came to an abrupt stop, slightly stumbling as he turned around. He had a gun in his hand and instantly tried to find a target to start firing. He got off one wild shot before Recker finished him off.

With him out of the way, Recker hurried over to the door. He took a peek inside the opened door, not seeing anything of note right off the bat. He still heard gunfire, though. It seemed like a little less than before, giving him the impression that one of the robbers had gone down.

As Recker slowly and cautiously moved through the building, he kept an eye out for any surprises. Though he knew there were only four robbers to begin with, he couldn't say for certain as to whether there was anybody already in there waiting for them.

As he kept moving, all the gunfire was coming from one area. Recker continued in that direction. Eventually, he saw the back of one of the men. He was at the edge of the wall, periodically taking shots, then taking cover behind the corner of the wall.

Recker had a clear line of sight on him. As the man took a couple more shots, Recker opened up on him, drilling him with a few rounds to the chest. As he fell to the ground, the last remaining member of the group rushed into the open area from a hallway, concerned about what just happened to his buddy.

The man had no idea where Recker was, though, and started firing blindly. Sometimes that was the most dangerous kind. Recker dropped to the floor to take cover. But the man was so focused on shooting at whoever was there, that he made himself vulnerable to Haley. With the hallway now clear, Haley quickly approached the man and fired a couple rounds that dropped the man.

With the coast seemingly clear, Recker stood up. Both he and Haley walked around the place to survey the damage.

"You got started a little early," Recker said.

"One of them must have noticed me coming up on the back door. Popped off a round at me."

After they cleared the building and found no one else to be there, they did their usual routine, and started taking pictures of the dead men. They also started searching the building, hoping to find any of their previous scores. They came up empty on that front, though. They then found the bag the robbers had taken. They laid out everything on a table. It was only diamonds.

"Looks like we got them," Haley said.

Recker nodded. "Seems like it."

Content with how things were, they put the diamonds back in the bag. They'd figure out a way to get it back to the jewelry store. But first, they put a call in to Jones to let him know the situation was under control and taken care of.

"Hey, David. Just wanted to tell you everything's good. We got the diamonds and these guys are out of commission."

"It appears to be a job well done," Jones said.

"We'll bring the diamonds back and figure out how to get them back to the owners."

"Excellent."

"Guess now we can concentrate on other things now that this is wrapped up."

"Uh, I wouldn't be too sure of that."

"What? Why not?"

"Because I'm not sure you've got who you think you do."

"What do you mean?" Recker asked.

"Because another robbery just went down twenty minutes ago."

Recker glanced at Haley, a little stunned at hearing the news. "What kind of robbery?"

"Jewelry store. Only diamonds taken. Three men."

Recker sighed in frustration, then rubbed his forehead. "What's going on here?"

"From my instincts, and this is only a guess, I'd say the people you've got there are not the people we've been looking for."

Recker looked down at one of the dead men. "Then who are they?"

"I guess that is the question, isn't it?"

"Maybe the people that did this new robbery you're talking about are copycats."

"I guess it's theoretically possible."

"But not likely?"

"Why don't you come back to the office and we can

start putting everything together to analyze it. Then we can come to a conclusion."

Recker took a deep breath. He could tell by the sound of his friend's voice that he had something convincing that would support his point of view. Recker's brief happiness at concluding the job was now dashed, assuming they had the wrong crew lying there on the floor. He looked at Haley and shook his head, feeling like they'd been played somehow.

"What the hell is going on here?"

15

Instead of taking the bag of diamonds with them, and figuring out how to return it later, Recker just left the bag there. Jones left an anonymous tip with the police department about hearing gunshots at that location. When the police arrived, they'd find the bag and return it through proper channels.

Besides, they had other things to worry about at the moment. Recker and Haley rushed straight back to the office, wanting to know what was going on with this latest robbery. They barged into the office, with Jones swiveling his chair around to face them as they entered the room.

"What's going on here?" Recker asked.

"It's just as I told you," Jones answered. "Another robbery went down."

"Where?"

Jones pointed to the screen on the wall, where he

was starting to project everything. There was a red circle on a map to indicate where the robbery happened.

"It happened here."

"Can you circle where all the other robberies went down?"

Jones nodded and immediately did as was requested. "Here are the other three. I also circled today's other robbery. You'll see that is the blue circle."

"Monty's Jewelry is completely across town from this other robbery today," Haley said.

"How do you know we got the wrong ones?" Recker asked.

"There were four men you went after today," Jones replied. "There were three with this one that we missed."

"Not exactly foolproof evidence."

"No, but there's also the fact that I ran the license plate on the white car you guys were following."

"Stolen?"

Jones shook his head. "No. It came back to Stephen Sneed."

Recker glared at him, like he was waiting for a bit more information. "And? Is that significant? Who's Stephen Sneed?"

"Because he was the driver of the white car. It was his."

Recker slightly tilted his head back. He could already see it.

"The guy used his own car to do the job?" Haley asked.

"That's correct," Jones answered.

Recker then moved his head around until he lowered it and looked at the ground. He knew Jones was right. That was all the information that he needed.

"I'm assuming you know what I'm referring to."

Recker sighed. "The other robberies all used stolen cars."

Jones put his index finger in the air. "And, I was already able to get a license plate photo off a nearby camera where the car was parked on this new robbery."

"And you ran it?"

"I did. It comes back as stolen."

Recker closed his eyes, then rubbed his forehead, before running his hands down his face.

"So, what... it's just some kind of coincidence that these two crews struck at the same time?" Haley asked. "Or near the same time?"

"You know I don't believe in those," Recker replied.

"Coordinated?"

"Something's rotten in Denmark."

Recker could only shake his head, for what seemed like a really long time. He then started pacing around the office, periodically looking back up at the screen on the wall.

"Do we know anything about the guys we took down?" Recker asked.

Jones nodded. "We do. I'll put them on the screen now."

As the four faces appeared on the screen, Recker stopped and walked over in front of it to get a better look. There was Sneed on the top left of the screen. The other three pictures were next to his.

"What do we know about them?"

"All have criminal records," Jones answered.

Recker read the information that was on the screen. He had some reservations.

"Only one that's been arrested for robbery." He then pointed to the picture next to Sneed's. "This guy."

"The rest have minor convictions," Haley said.

"That would explain why some of them seemed jumpy when we ran into them." Recker pointed to Sneed's picture. "Especially this guy. He looked like he was about to wet himself when he ran out the door."

Recker stared down at the floor for a minute, thinking things over. There was a lot going on here.

"We should've stayed at that building for a while."

"Why?" Haley asked.

"It had to be a meeting place."

"With who?"

"I don't know," Recker said. "Somebody bigger. Look at these guys. Outside of one, they don't really have the chops for all this."

"Well, they did do it," Jones said.

Recker wasn't buying it. "But look at their records.

Three of them don't have a history of this type of stuff. What do they know about getting rid of diamonds?"

"The fourth guy?"

"Yeah, maybe he's the ringleader, but I have a hard time believing he'd get an inexperienced crew. We got any type of value yet on the stuff that was stolen?"

"Not determined yet," Jones replied. "On either location."

"You think someone hired these guys?" Haley asked. "Then was going to meet up with them?"

Recker shrugged. "It's a theory."

"It wouldn't matter much now," Jones said. "If they're not the ones we were looking for, the matter is concluded."

Recker disagreed. "It's not concluded. I don't think this is some random coincidence."

Jones looked at him like he was going off the deep end. "You think two robberies were planned?"

"That's not what I'm saying."

"Then what are you saying?"

Recker wasn't totally sure in his own mind, but just thought it was too convenient that another diamond robbery happened to go down at roughly the same time. He folded his arms across his chest as he continued to stare at the screen. He turned around to face Jones.

"What are the odds? We're looking for diamond robbers, and there's no activity for what, a week? Whatever it is? Then all of a sudden, two go down on the same day, just minutes apart, one across town from the other? That doesn't smell fishy to you?"

"It could be just one of those things."

Recker shook his head. He wasn't having any of that. It wasn't just one of those things. And it wasn't just one of those coincidences that he didn't usually buy anyway. This was more. He knew it.

"This is connected."

"I just asked you if you thought the two robberies were planned," Jones said.

"I don't mean like that."

"You think one was specifically made to draw us out," Haley said. "Don't you?"

Recker nodded. "That's what I think."

"That takes some planning."

"It does."

"Almost sounds ludicrous," Jones said. "And... far-fetched?"

"How so?" Recker asked.

"One, they'd have to be counting on us to somehow find out about this first robbery."

"Which we did."

"But that's putting a lot of faith into a huge unknown."

"Think about it. That's why Trae kept hearing about it from so many sources. Somebody wanted us to know that. This person started spreading it every-where, knowing we have sources on the street, wanting it to get back to us."

Jones shook his hand a little, not sure he bought it. "A little shaky, I think."

"If you want word to get back to us, you tell anyone and everyone. Somebody out there's gonna have loose lips."

"OK, let's just say I buy that. And I'm not saying I do. But let's just suppose. Who and why?"

"The why is easy," Recker answered. "They wanted us covering a different robbery. Somewhere far away. That way when they struck at their real location, they wouldn't have to worry about us."

"These other guys were offered up on a silver platter," Haley said. "They set those guys up, hoping we'd take them out."

"I think it makes sense."

"I'm buying it."

"Who?" Jones asked. "Who would be able to pull that off? And how would they know specifically about us?"

"That parts easy," Recker replied. "We obviously had to talk to them about it. That cuts down the possibilities to just a couple."

"D'Amonico, Vervaat, and Sharma," Haley said. "It's gotta be one of those three."

"I think it's pretty likely. They're the ones we stepped up the pressure with the most. They all know we're on this. If they were scared of us messing up their next job, they set up a fake job, hoped that we'd get an ear on it, and take it. It leaves the real job wide open."

"Pretty smart, actually."

"It is."

"I can understand your logic," Jones said. "I'm not sure I'm there yet."

"It makes sense," Recker replied.

"Maybe. So you're telling me one of these three hired these four, hoping they'd get caught or killed?"

"I don't know about that part. Maybe he was hoping they'd get away with it. Maybe he didn't really care either way. I think the only real intention was to keep us busy long enough for the real job to get completed. Whatever happened with these guys I don't think was much of a consideration. They were only there to be decoys. That's it."

"I'm still not sold on it, but I can see the logic of it. Whether that's the case or not, what's next?"

Recker glanced at Haley. "Before, we knocked on some doors."

"Yeah, we did," his partner replied.

"Now, let's kick them in."

16

Before Recker and Haley embarked on anything, they wanted to make sure they had the latest information. That meant waiting until they had all the facts on the latest two robberies. Once they finally had that, then they could go kick some doors in. Literally or otherwise.

They were all stewing around the office, waiting for that final word to come in. Then Jones got it. He started snapping his fingers.

"Here we go."

Recker and Haley rushed over to his position.

"What do we got?" Recker asked.

"First up, we have the gentlemen who are no longer with us, thanks to you."

Recker smirked. "Sorry."

"Looks like the value of the diamonds they took was about ten thousand dollars."

"Nothing to sneeze at," Haley said.

"But not keeping with the pattern the other robberies set," Recker replied. "Each one increased in value."

Jones put his finger in the air to let him continue. "The one we missed out on, the value was seventy-five thousand dollars."

Recker and Haley glanced at each other.

"That's it," Recker said. "Increase in value. We missed them."

"Let's go for round two," Haley said.

"Before you do that," Jones said. "I have some additional thoughts."

"Can you make them quick?" Recker asked.

"Why, itchy trigger finger?"

Recker smiled, then wiggled his fingers. "Maybe."

Jones rolled his eyes. "If this big theory of yours is true, and one of these guys is behind this. Why not just call everything off? If they know you're coming, why risk it?"

It was a fair point, Recker thought. But he had an answer. "Maybe they couldn't? Maybe everything was already in the works. Maybe all these jobs had already been set up weeks ago."

"Only takes a minute to call it off."

"Not if you've already spent some of the money."

Jones scrunched his eyebrows together, not sure of his meaning. "Spent it?"

"What if you've already set up a buyer for these?

You've already accepted payment? Or you've already got things in motion? Maybe you've already paid people who are working in the background. You don't want that to go to waste. So you still have to go through with it. But you make alternative plans."

"Which is where that other crew comes in," Haley said.

"That's my theory."

Jones could see the merit in his thinking. "So what are your plans today?"

"Step up the pressure," Recker answered. "We're gonna kick in some doors and let them know we know what they're up to."

"To all three of them?"

"Sure. One of them is behind this. I know it. I just don't know which one. Let's see which one of them cracks. One of them will."

"Sure of that, are you?"

Recker grinned. "Yep. They can't resist my charm."

"Oh, is that what we're calling it these days? Charm?"

"Sure. Why not?"

"What if none of them cracks? What if you don't get the answer that you're looking for?"

"Well, that's the thing. You don't always get that answer right away. But like this other job they set up, that was a response to the last time we visited. If we go in guns blazing, they'll be another response. Don't know when or where, but there'll be one."

"Question is, will it be one that we see coming?" Jones asked. "We didn't with this one. What if we don't with the next one either?"

"There's only so many times you can pull tricks before you make a mistake somewhere. Sooner or later, you'll trip yourself up. This is no different. If we keep up the pressure, they'll make a mistake. And we'll be there when they do."

"Fair enough."

Recker and Haley left the office, with their first order of business being Charles D'Amonico. Considering it was the middle of the day, they assumed they would find D'Amonico at his place of business. It was a larger business than one would expect. There was a group of offices on one side of the building, which was attached to a warehouse, most likely where they kept all the goods they were bringing in or exporting. It was probably close to a thirty thousand square foot building. Recker and Haley walked into the office, and immediately were greeted by a secretary.

"Can I help you?"

"Charles D'Amonico," Recker answered.

"Are you expected?"

"Oh, yes."

"Well he's in a meeting right now. Are you on the schedule?"

"Uh, no, this is an emergency."

A worried look appeared on her face. "Oh. Is something wrong with his family or something?"

"No."

"Can I ask what you're here for, then?"

"Business," Recker replied.

"Can I have your name? I'll tell him you're here."

"We'll just wait for him to be done."

While the secretary was focused on Recker, Haley had walked around the other side of the desk and snooped around. He saw a list on the desk with office numbers and phone numbers.

"210," Haley said.

The secretary snapped her head around to him. "Hey! You can't do that!"

"I just did."

Recker walked out of the lobby and into a hallway.

"Hey, you can't go down that way!"

Recker paid her no mind as she raced over to him to try to stop him. Haley walked in the same direction, though a little bit behind them.

"You're not authorized to be back here," the secretary said. "I have to approve everyone first."

"So approve me," Recker replied.

"But you're not on the schedule."

"He knows me."

"But he's in a meeting."

"I think the meeting's over."

They finally arrived at D'Amonico's office and Recker opened the door. There were two other men sitting in chairs across from D'Amonico, who was behind his desk. He instantly got a worried look on his face as he saw the two familiar men standing there in the doorway.

"I'm sorry Mr. D'Amonico, they just barged right in. I couldn't stop them."

D'Amonico just kind of waved her off, knowing there was nothing she could have done.

"Looks like your meeting's over," Recker said.

"What's the meaning of this?" one of the other men asked.

"Are you dirty too?"

"Excuse me?"

"Yeah, you're excused. You and the other guy. Get out of here before I start looking into your shady dealings too."

"Who are you?"

"If you don't get out of here in two seconds, I'll be your worst nightmare."

D'Amonico, having dealt with them before, wasn't really interested in having a scene there. Especially in front of others. Though he really didn't want to deal with the two men, he didn't want them hassling his business associates.

"It's fine. It's fine. We can continue this later. Just give us the room right now."

Recker stood there, giving both of the men a smile as they exited the room.

"See you later."

The secretary wasn't quite sure what to do. "Should I...?"

"Go back to your desk?" Recker asked. "Yes, you should."

"It's fine," D'Amonico said. "Thank you. We're fine here."

After the secretary walked out of the room, Recker closed the door, then glared at D'Amonico, who seemed a little wary about what was coming.

Recker had a small grin on his face. "Looks like we got things to discuss."

17

As Recker and Haley stepped closer to the desk, D'Amonico put his hands up as if they were close to hitting him, and he was trying to stop them somehow. Recker and Haley then took a seat left by the former visitors that were there.

D'Amonico took a deep breath. "What are you guys doing here?"

"Just wanted another chat," Recker answered.

"There's nothing more to discuss than the last time we saw each other."

"Well that's just not true."

"Don't keep me waiting too long. I got things to do."

"Another diamond robbery went down yesterday. As a matter of fact, there were two of them."

D'Amonico faked a sorrowful expression. "That's too bad. So sorry to hear it. What's that got to do with me?"

"You set it up, didn't you?"

D'Amonico laughed. "What?! That's preposterous!"

"Is it? Didn't you send out two pairs of teams? One to throw us off the track and one doing the real job?"

"I assume you have some type of evidence to charge me with here?"

"No, no evidence," Recker replied. "Just my suspicions."

"Oh, well, as long as you have something concrete, then."

"This meeting is just to let you know we're coming for you."

"I'm shaking in my boots."

"You should be. Because when we get someone in our sights, we don't let go. You, and your entire organization, is going down."

D'Amonico closed his eyes, and sweat started pouring off his face. He wiped his forehead, looking like he was agonizing over something. He was starting to feel the heat.

"OK, look, I don't know what you two think I've got going on, but I can assure you, I don't have anything to do with any diamond robberies."

"Why should we believe that?" Haley asked.

D'Amonico threw his hands up. "Why would I?! I've been under investigation three times in the last five years. Yes, I've done some things that have skirted the law. I'm not denying that. But I'm clean now. I swear I am. Those investigations were hell on my family. Especially my kids."

"So we're supposed to just take your word that you're on the straight and narrow now?"

"Yes. Because I am. I promise you I'm doing nothing outside of the law. Especially these diamond robberies you're talking about."

"Your name did come up as someone to talk to about it," Recker said. "Since you import and export and all."

"Yes, a few years ago, I partook in some of that stuff. Again, I'm not denying that. That's probably why some people still think I'm in that business. But I'm not. I can't put my family through the aftermath of that stuff."

"Why should we believe that?"

"Check my books if you want. I'll let you look through everything. See if you find any discrepancies. Take a look around the property. See if you find anything that looks amiss. You have my permission to do whatever you want. I've got nothing to hide."

Recker and Haley glanced at each other. It was an offer they weren't quite expecting to hear. D'Amonico could see they still weren't convinced, and he needed to do a little extra.

"Look, that party you showed up at the other day? That was for my kids. They've had a tough time at school over the past few years. There's been teasing, bullying, all that stuff. It's been tough on them, hearing things about me. Other kids teasing them about me being a criminal, or going to jail, or all that stuff that kids sometimes say. I threw that party for them and invited a bunch of kids from their school to try and make things better for them. And it worked. They've been happier since. They've even made more friends. I wouldn't throw that away for whatever this is all about."

"Not even for the million dollars that have been taken so far?" Recker asked.

"Not for all the money in the world. I don't wanna say I don't care about any of it. I certainly hope nobody's gotten hurt in any of it. But whatever's going on there is not my concern. I've had a lot of amends to make for hurting my family in the way that I have over the years. And I'm not doing it anymore. I don't want to be in my sixties with a wife that divorced me and kids that don't wanna talk to me. I'm done with that. I'm just repairing my life now. That's it."

This wasn't quite how Recker was expecting this conversation to go down. But it was good. He tended to believe D'Amonico. He seemed to be speaking from the heart. And he didn't bat an eye when Recker gave him the wrong value amount of the diamonds stolen. He threw that million dollars out there, hoping D'Amonico would flinch, knowing the amount was wrong. He'd either correct Recker, or he'd make some facial expression inadvertently, giving off the vibe that he really did know what was going down. But

D'Amonico didn't flinch. He was either a really good liar, or honestly didn't know what was happening.

"Please, I can't take any more of your accusations," D'Amonico said. "The last time we spoke in front of my wife, and I had to assure her that I wasn't involved in anything you were talking about. I don't want to go through that again. It's been hell in trying to regain her trust. And I don't want my kids to think I'm back to old tricks again or anything. So please, whatever this diamond business is about, I assure you I have nothing to do with it."

"So you don't mind if we take a look around?" Recker asked.

"Be my guest. Look anywhere you want. If it'll help to put this behind me, I welcome your presence. Look in any office, the warehouses, outside, the books, whatever you want. You have my permission and blessing. As long as it puts me in the clear and I never have to worry about this again."

"Very welcoming of you."

"As I said, I just want my past behind me and to stay there. I'm not going to deny some of the things I've done. Luckily, I had some good lawyers, and I was able to escape any serious charges. But I'm done with that."

"It took three investigations? You didn't see the light after the first one?"

D'Amonico gestured with his hands. "What can I say? I was dumb. I thought it was a one-time thing. I was sloppy, foolish, I wouldn't make the same mistakes again. I could get away with it. I was obviously wrong. And dumb. And my family was there for me. As they were for the second time."

"The third time was different?" Haley asked.

D'Amonico took a deep breath, appearing to be genuinely affected by remembering it all. "My wife told me that she'd had enough. That if I was going to continue down that path, that she and the kids would not be a part of it. I, uh, took a good hard look at myself. Figured out what I really wanted in life. And it wasn't the extra money. It was my family. And I didn't want to lose them. We make a good living as it is. If you say these diamonds are worth a million, God bless whoever took them. Hopefully it helps them find whatever peace they're looking for. But it's not me."

Recker and Haley continued talking with D'Amonico for a little while, just to make sure he really was genuine in his remorse. They also wanted to see if they could trip him up somewhere, make him change his story somewhere along the line. But the man never wavered in his innocence. He sure made a compelling case. One that Recker and Haley both believed.

Still, they didn't just blindly take his word for it. D'Amonico offered the facilities to them, and they took him up on the offer. Recker and Haley wandered around, taking a look absolutely everywhere. There was no office or room that was unavailable to them. They even talked to a few employees, and while they didn't say exactly what they were looking for, they didn't get the impression that anyone knew of any improprieties that were going on. Everything seemed to be on the up and up.

When they were done, they met back up with D'Amonico in his office.

"I take it you're satisfied?"

"For now," Recker answered.

"Didn't find anything, did you?"

"Not yet."

"Because there is nothing to find. I've gone out of my way to be accommodating. Now please, can you please just leave me alone?"

"As long as we don't find any evidence that leads us back here, you probably won't see us again," Recker replied.

"Well thank goodness for that."

"Thanks for your time. We'll see ourselves out."

D'Amonico breathed a sigh of relief as the two men left his office, hopeful that he would never see them again. Once Recker and Haley reached their car, they discussed their next steps.

"I don't think he's our guy," Haley said.

Recker looked back at the building. "No, I don't think so either."

"I believed him. Unless he's really good."

"He might be. Really good, that is. But I didn't get the impression he was lying to us. Especially about his family. It looked like that really moved him. And he never flinched when I told him about the million dollars."

"Not even close to that," Haley said.

"I think we're barking up the wrong tree with him."

"I agree."

Recker's thoughts turned to Vervaat. "Well, we got one more to check off the list."

"I'm sure he'll be thrilled to see us."

Recker smiled. "Oh, I'm sure he will."

18

Recker and Haley were on the road, driving to have a meeting with Damien Vervaat. Unlike D'Amonico, Vervaat wasn't in his office every day. Quite often, he'd make deals wherever it was possible. The park, a back alley, in a pool hall, a bar, standing on a corner, or in his office. He just didn't care where. And quite often, with some of the people he was meeting, he didn't want them in his office, anyway.

So there wasn't a guarantee that Recker and Haley would find him there. They were about halfway to Vervaat's office when they got a call from Jones.

"Have you reached his office yet?" Jones asked.

"No, we're about twenty minutes from it," Recker replied. "Why, what's up?"

"Your friend, Mr. Sharma, that's what's up."

"No friend of mine."

"Regardless, he now seems to have a fascination with you."

Recker smiled. "Who doesn't?"

"Indeed. Anyway, he called your personal service and left a message for you."

"You talk to him?"

"I clearly said he called your personal service."

"Isn't that you?"

"I'll ignore that," Jones said. "He called the number you left him."

"So what'd he say?"

"I'll just play it for you so you can listen to it yourself."

Recker pulled over to the side of the road so he wasn't distracted and could fully concentrate on what was being said. Jones then played the message.

It was Sharma's voice. "This is for The Silencer. I may have some news for you. In regards to our previous conversation, I understand you are unwilling to make that concession, and that's fine. I will not ask for that again. But I do have a name that may interest you. I have been doing some digging, and I've got a name for someone who is in the crew that you are looking for. If you are interested, I could provide that name to you. Call me back at this number, if you please."

Recker and Haley looked at each other once the message was done.

"Man, talk about shady characters," Haley said. "That guy's definitely one."

"Yeah."

"I wasn't sure if that would alter your plans at the moment," Jones said.

"Well, in order to set something up with him, I'd have to come back to the office and call him," Recker replied. "Because I'm not giving him this number. Seems like we'd be doing a lot of running around."

"But if he's got a name...?"

"I know, I know. Let's just continue what we're doing now. We'll meet with Vervaat. Then when we get back, I'll call Sharma."

"What if the name Sharma gives you, you could then present to Vervaat?"

"And what if he gives me slop?"

"True point."

"Hey, if he gives me something worthwhile, I can always come back. But I don't want to waste half the day just driving around and not get anywhere."

"Understood. Would you like me to call Sharma on your behalf?" Jones asked.

"No. I don't want him knowing there's more of us."

"OK. Good luck with your talk."

Recker pulled back onto the road and continued driving towards Vervaat's office. It was located on the edge of the city. It was only a four-story building. Nothing too big or grand. There were dozens of other small businesses and offices located within it. Along the way, Haley found a number associated with Vervaat's office and called it, verifying that the boss was there. There'd be no sense in continuing in that direction if the man wasn't even there that day. If he wasn't, they'd just switch gears and try Vervaat at his home. Luckily, they didn't have to.

Once they made their way up to the fourth floor, Recker and Haley went directly to Vervaat's office. It was a relatively small office. There was the secretary's desk, and a few chairs around the room for people to wait, and then the door to what they assumed was Vervaat's office. There didn't appear to be any other rooms or hallways or anything. They were once again greeted by a secretary.

"Why do these guys go to such great lengths to act legit?" Recker whispered to his partner.

"Excuse me?" the secretary asked.

"Oh, nothing. A private thing. We're here to see Damien Vervaat."

"Is he expecting you?"

"Same questions too," Haley said.

"What?"

"Nothing."

"First, is there any other way out of here?" Recker asked.

"Any other way out?"

"Like, to get out of here."

"We're on the fourth floor."

Recker grinned. "I mean, is that door the only way

in and out of here? Is there a back door that leads to a hallway or something?"

The secretary looked mightily confused and had no idea where this conversation was heading. Recker just wanted to make sure nobody could duck out the back way if Vervaat knew they were out there.

"Uh, no, that's the only door to the office."

Recker smiled. "Great. Just what I wanted to know."

"OOK."

"And is anyone else in there with him? I mean, any other meeting or anything?"

"No, no one."

"Fantastic."

"OK, should I... I mean, who should I say is here?"

"Oh, just tell him Mr. Silencer."

The secretary looked at him like he was putting her on. The name meant nothing to her, but she knew that couldn't have been his last name.

"Is that really your last name?"

Recker smirked. "The one that I was born with. Memorable and catchy, isn't it?"

The secretary still gave him a look like she wasn't sure if this was some type of elaborate prank. Still, she buzzed into the office.

"Yes?" Vervaat asked.

"Um, there is someone here to see you."

"There is? Who is it?"

"Someone named... Mr. Silencer?"

"What?!"

"That's who he said."

The secretary wasn't paying a lick of attention to Haley, who had backed away from Recker. Since the secretary was focused on Recker, Haley slipped over to the office door.

"Tell him I'm in a meeting," Vervaat said.

Haley slowly turned the handle and pushed it open. He shook his head as he saw Vervaat sitting there behind the desk.

"Such a lie. You're not doing anything."

Vervaat jumped up, obviously flustered, and stumbled around as he took a couple of tries to hang up his phone.

"What are you doing here? You can't be here."

"Well here I am," Haley replied.

Recker then joined his partner by the door. "There he is."

"Oh no," Vervaat said.

As Recker and Haley stepped inside the office, the secretary came over, trying to do something to solve the problem.

"You guys can't..."

Recker put his finger up to his lips. "This is very important. We can't be disturbed in here OK? So if anyone else comes in, it'll ruin the whole deal."

"What deal?" the secretary asked.

"It's very hush-hush. Really secretive. Your boss might be able to give you a really nice year-end bonus if it goes through."

"Oh."

"So we're gonna need some time to sort through some things, OK?"

"OK."

"No phone calls, OK?"

"Sure."

Recker smiled at her. "Thank you. We'll be out soon."

As the secretary went back to her desk, Recker closed and locked the door.

"That should give us some privacy."

"What do you two want?" Vervaat asked.

"Before we get to that, does she actually do anything? Or is it just for show?"

"I'm a very important businessman, you know. I have a lot of clients, people who need meetings, things like that. I need someone to make appointments, write things down, things like that."

"Oh. OK. How's the seventy-five thousand dollars holding up?"

"What?"

"The latest diamond heist," Recker said. "Get your cut yet?"

"Back to that again, are you? I assure you, I have no idea what you're talking about."

"Shame about the second crew," Haley said.

"What second crew?" Vervaat asked.

"The ones that took that ten grand from Monty's Jewelry. Sorry they didn't make it."

"Oh, didn't they?"

"But you probably knew that anyway, right?" Recker said.

Vervaat's face wasn't giving anything away. "I have no idea."

"They're all dead. But we're not telling you anything you don't already know, are we?"

"As a matter of fact, it's the first I'm hearing about it."

"You're lying straight to our faces."

"I'm not. Why would I?"

"Because you're trying to keep your involvement a secret?"

Vervaat shook his head. "I have so many other things going on, I don't have time to plot out these robberies that you think I'm involved with."

"Like what?" Recker asked.

"What?"

"Like what? What other things do you have going on?"

"I don't have to tell you that! That's private business."

"Yeah, well, those robberies are our business, and I think you're involved up to your neck."

Vervaat wasn't cracking no matter how much Recker leaned on him.

"I don't see any evidence in your hands. You know why that is? Because you don't have any!"

"I don't need evidence to know something. And you're guilty. I can feel it."

Vervaat stuck his wrists out. "Feel free to lock me up and arrest me anytime you feel like it."

"I'll do worse than that."

Vervaat rolled his eyes. "Look, I'm getting tired of these accusations and insinuations. If you have something concrete that implicates me, show it to me. If not, get out of here. I have things to do."

"You come across as someone who's hiding something."

"I don't care."

"We could beat it out of you," Recker said.

"You could, but you won't. You know why? Because you would've done it already. And also, it wouldn't get you anywhere."

"What about Stephen Sneed?"

"Who?!"

"Stephen Sneed. He was one of the guys that got killed in the second robbery. The one you planted hoping we'd be there so the other one could go off without a hitch."

A devilish smile formed on Vervaat's face. "Well wouldn't that be a brilliant piece of planning if I did?"

"He's been seen here, you know."

"Preposterous. He's never been seen here. He's never been inside this building."

"How do you know that?" Recker asked.

"Because I've never met him."

"Then how do you know he's never been here?"

"OK, I assume he's never been in this office. Satisfied?"

"Not really."

"I'm afraid there's really nothing else I can tell you."

"You can tell me how you don't know a man that you were photographed as being in his car," Recker said. "Security camera footage picked you up. Sitting in the passenger seat. In his white car. You know, the one with the small..."

Haley snapped his fingers. "Yeah, the car's very unforgettable with the marks on it."

"I'd like to see pictures," Vervaat said.

Recker patted his pockets. "Don't seem to have them with me at the moment."

Vervaat laughed. "You're really quite bad at this, you know that? I mean, do you think I just fell off the turnip truck yesterday? You come in here with all these accusations, not one shred of evidence or proof that I'm involved, and you think I'm just going to crumble and admit to everything because you're standing in front of me? Please!"

"Don't work that way, huh?"

"No, it doesn't."

"You're too sophisticated for that. Been through this type of thing too many times, right? You're experienced in what to say."

"It's easy to say the right thing when you're in the clear."

"You still haven't explained the white car," Haley said. "It's clearly you in there. And that mark?"

"So there's a small dent in the door," Vervaat replied. "So what? Do you know how many white cars out there have dents in them? Probably a thousand."

Haley grinned. "Yeah. You're probably right."

Recker had heard all he needed to. They got their man. "You know what? We've taken up too much of your time already. You're obviously not going to confess to anything, and we can't prove anything, at least not yet, so I guess we're just gonna have to call it a draw for the moment."

Vervaat's smile widened, feeling like he had one-upped the two men. "Probably a good idea."

"We won't take up any more of your precious time. We can see your schedule is packed."

Recker and Haley bid the man goodbye, then left the office. Once they got out of the building entirely, they went back to their car to call Jones.

"Did you hear what I did?" Recker asked.

"Sure did," Haley replied. "I can't say I noticed whether there was a small dent in that car."

"Yeah, neither did I. Too much else going on."

"That was pretty smart leading him in that direction."

"I just figured he wasn't going to identify the color of the car or anything. He's too smart for that. We had to lead him there in some other way."

Jones answered the video call. "Is your meeting

over?"

"It is," Recker answered. "Do you happen to have pictures of Sneed's car when you were digging up all the info on them?"

"The white car?"

"That's Sneed's, isn't it?"

"Yes, but what do you need?"

"We need to know if there's a small dent in the door."

"Which door?" Jones asked.

"Don't know. Doesn't matter which one."

"Oh. OK." Jones began looking through the file he had put together so far. "Let's see... huh. There it is."

"There's what?"

"A small dent on the back door on the passenger side."

"So there is one there?"

"I'm looking at the security footage from Monty's Jewelry. The dent is plainly visible. It's right there."

Recker started smiling.

"Why are you looking like that?" Jones asked.

"Because that's what we needed. That's the connection."

"I don't follow you."

"You had to be there. We'll fill you in once we get back to the office."

"I feel like I'm missing something."

"You are," Recker said. "But don't worry. We're on the right track."

19

When Recker and Haley got back to the office, they filled their partner in on the meeting with Vervaat.

"So you're telling me he just offered up the dent? Just like that?"

"Well, it wasn't just like that," Recker replied. "We kind of led him in that direction. We said there was a mark that identified the car. We didn't say it was a dent. Could've been a sticker, something with the paint job, rust, anything. He must have thought we were talking about the dent to begin with."

"Smart. Unfortunately, that doesn't really prove what we hope it does."

"How doesn't it? It means he knows Sneed. He knows the car."

"It proves he knows that set of robbers. It still

doesn't provide a connection to the ones we're after regardless of whether we think it does. There's no proof to connect them. And it doesn't even connect him to Monty's Jewelry. Just because he knows Sneed doesn't mean he's the one that ordered him to go there."

"Well, there's the whole lying thing," Haley said. "That kind of makes it iffy."

"No doubt. And to be clear, I'm not saying I don't believe he's involved. I'm just saying the evidence is not there yet. He could have met with Sneed about something completely unrelated."

"What are the odds of that?"

"Admittedly, probably low," Jones said. "But that doesn't mean the possibility doesn't exist."

"But it means we can dig further into Sneed's background," Recker said. "There has to be something that links the two of them together. We have to find that link."

Jones nodded. "I'll get right on it. Oh, what did you want to do about Sharma?"

"Almost forgot about that. I'll call him back. Maybe he's got something."

"Only thing he's got is some snake oil to sell you," Haley said. "What's the thing they did back in the day? Some traveling doctor on a wagon or something selling medicine to cure you, except it was... I don't even know."

"Usually some elixir of nonsense," Recker replied.

"I get the feeling Sharma would've fit right in back then."

Recker laughed. "Probably so."

He then took the phone off the desk and called Sharma, who picked up after the third ring.

"I was hoping you would call back."

"This isn't a social call," Recker said. "You mentioned having a name."

"I did. But unfortunately, I am a businessman. That name comes at a cost."

"What is it?"

"Let's meet in person and talk about it."

"I'd rather just talk here."

"I'd rather not," Sharma replied. "I find in-person meetings to be much more effective in making sure there is a proper exchange of thoughts and ideas. That way everyone winds up getting what they want."

"OK. I can meet with you somewhere. But I'm going to warn you. If this is some sort of trick, you are going to have one unhappy camper on your hands."

"I understand. There will be no tricks."

"Just so we're clear, above all else, my time is valuable. And I hate having it wasted. So when I feel that it is, I become a raging bull that's unstoppable. I hope that's clear."

"Oh, it very much is. Crystal."

"Where would you like to meet?" Recker asked. "And before you say anything, I'm not meeting inside any buildings or closed off spaces. It'll be outside and in public."

"You play things very carefully."

"Only with people I don't know and trust."

"I was going to suggest the same thing anyway. We can meet at a park, if you like? Plenty of open space, children around, people, and no worries of anyone doing anything silly."

"Sounds fine."

"How about we make it three hours from now?"

"How about we make it now," Recker answered.

"Well I did have some other business to attend to first."

"I can make it now or not at all."

"Very well. I can push my other appointments until later."

Sharma then said the name of the park he wanted to meet at. Recker had no objections with the place, so they agreed to meet. After hanging up, Recker and Haley got ready.

"You sure this is a good idea," Haley said.

"One of the reasons I insisted on now was... less time for him to prepare for a setup. That park is about forty-five minutes away from us. We might be able to get there ahead of time. You keep your eyes on us from a distance. You know what to look for."

"It could be that he actually does have something useful for us," Jones said.

"He might," Recker replied. "But it's not going to come to us without a cost."

"I just hope he's not wasting our time," Haley said.

"We'll find out soon enough."

Recker and Haley quickly left the office, wanting to get to the park before Sharma and his men did. Though they didn't think Sharma was setting them up for something, they couldn't outright discount the idea. But in the unlikely event that Sharma did have something shady planned, Recker wanted Haley out there scouting around. If there was something fishy going on, Haley would find it.

As they drove to the meeting place, Recker kept thinking about what the information would cost. He knew Sharma wasn't going to just give it away for free. As his own words stated, he was a businessman. And a businessman would always get something if he was holding something valuable. It didn't have to be money. But it could be something equally as good, if not better. Recker just wasn't sure what that something would be. Sharma already knew that the meeting with Vincent was off the table. Recker wasn't sure what else there was that Sharma would want. He knew he'd find out soon enough, though.

To their satisfaction, Recker and Haley did beat the others to the park. It was a fairly small park. There was one walking trail, a few baseball and soccer fields, and a skating area. There was also a large playground right in the middle of everything, along with some benches and covered pavilion areas.

Since it didn't look like Sharma had arrived yet, Recker took a seat on one of the benches facing the playground. There were probably a dozen children on it, with their parents or grandparents all nearby watching, encouraging the smaller ones. A slight smile crept over Recker's face as he watched a couple of the children. There was something soothing and calming over watching the innocence of a child playing. And it was a welcome relief from the usual environments he found himself in.

Moments like this were good for him. It served as a reminder of why he did what he did. To protect people like that, the children, the parents, the grandparents, and make sure they didn't get caught up in all the bad that was going on out there.

It didn't take Sharma too much longer to show up. Since it wasn't a big park, it didn't take him a lot of looking to find Recker. Once Sharma found him, he walked over to the bench. Recker picked him up out of the corner of his eye and watched him come. Sharma was alone, though Recker did notice a few of the guards waiting by the parked car.

"Looks like we're clear," Haley said into Recker's earpiece.

Recker tapped his ear to confirm he got the message. He turned his head back to the kids on the playground as Sharma walked over and sat down next to him.

"One of the most pleasant sounds in the world, don't you agree?"

"What's that?" Recker said.

"A child's laughter. One of the most pure things one can imagine."

"Didn't peg you as someone who loves kids. Have any?"

"No. Not as of yet. Do you?"

"Nope. Let's get down to business. You said you had a name."

"I do," Sharma said. "But as I mentioned to you, that name comes with a cost."

"What is it?"

"I would like use of your services."

"That's a non-starter," Recker said.

"Wouldn't have to be permanent."

"I work for me. Nobody else."

"But your arrangement with Vincent would say otherwise."

"Look, I don't know what you hear, but I don't work for him. Sometimes our situations might align in the same direction, but that's all. If he steps over the line or gets in my way, I'll deal with him the same way I deal with anyone else. The important part in the relationship that Vincent and I have is he sees the value in not crossing me."

"It sounds as if you would like the information for free."

"We all know that's not the way this world works," Recker replied. "If there's something that doesn't have a monetary value attached to it, it's something we can discuss. But anything involving a dollar amount, or my services, is an instant no-go. And a waste of my time."

"Perhaps you would like to throw something out at me. I would like to hear your definition of valuable."

"Sometimes people in my line of work hear things. Something that can be useful to a person like you. Whether that's a rival gang coming in, or someone who has their sights set on you. Maybe something like that would be of interest to know what's coming."

"Perhaps it would. But it sounds like that's a favor that might not be repaid for quite a long time."

"Could be."

"How would I know there is not an expiration date attached to it?"

"I don't put expiration dates on my favors," Recker answered.

"Good to know. It sounds like I don't have much of a bargaining position with you."

"Sure you do. You can take it or leave it."

"You appear to be a man quite used to getting your way."

"Usually. But that's only because I'm confident in my abilities to get what I need, anyway. Doing a deal... I just get it faster."

"Say I agree to your terms. A name for a favor to be repaid further down the line. Is that agreeable to you?"

"Depends on the name. Because if you give me a name that I already know about, this whole conversation's been a waste of time. And I've already told you how I feel about that."

"It seems as if you hold all the cards. How do I know you won't hear the name and pretend like it's one you already know about?"

"Because I'm not in the habit of stiffing people," Recker said.

"Still a risk I'm taking on my part."

"Then say half of it. If I know it, I'll say the other half."

"Sounds reasonable."

"The name I have for you begins with Stephen."

"If his last name also starts with an S, you're wasting your time. I already know about him. Plus, he's dead."

A small smile came over Sharma's face. "Ah, I see you do know about Mr. Sneed's unfortunate demise."

Recker shrugged. "Depends on what you call unfortunate, I guess. In any case, like I said, he's dead. Makes no difference now."

"Am I to assume you were the one to put him in his now unenviable position?"

Recker wasn't about to admit anything, especially to a man like Sharma. That would be an admission he was sure he'd come to regret at some point in time.

Likely when he was in a vulnerable position. No, he wouldn't give Sharma anything to work with that could be used against him.

"I don't really know the circumstances. But it doesn't really matter, does it? He's dead. Nothing else matters."

"I would not be so sure about that," Sharma said. "Even dead men have a way of telling us things."

"And what would that be?"

"A connection I have found. Follow the trail. It will lead you to where you want to go."

Recker wasn't learning anything new. And he was beginning to feel like this was a monumental waste of his time. Haley was right. Sharma was a snake-oil salesman. He didn't have anything. At least, nothing useful. But he would pretend like he did. He'd pretend like he was a bigger player than he actually was. He was itching to move up in the underworld. To improve his position and standing. And he'd do just about anything to get there. That much was clear. But it was equally clear that he was more like a con man, promising things that he could never deliver. And he was having no more of it.

Recker stood up. He wasn't going to waste anymore time there. "Well, thanks for the chat. I think we're done here, though."

"Don't you want to know where Sneed's trail leads?"

"I already know where it leads," Recker replied.

"Straight to the doorsteps of someone named Damien Vervaat."

Sharma grinned. But he closed his eyes for a moment, then shook his head. "I'm afraid not."

Recker scrunched his face together, sure the man was pulling his leg.

"By the look on your face, it appears I've said something you already didn't know. Finally."

Recker slowly sat back down, staring at his company. "What do you mean, no?"

"If they were breadcrumbs, you would see Mr. Sneed's trail lead right up to the door of a man named Charles D'Amonico. He is a..."

"I know the name."

"Ah."

"How do you figure Sneed's lined up with him?"

"Mr. Sneed was in D'Amonico's employment as recently as several weeks ago."

"How do you know this?"

Sharma smiled. "How does one know anything? Because I did business with Mr. D'Amonico."

"When?"

"As I said, several weeks ago."

"What kind of business?"

Sharma grinned and let out a slight, but quickly fading laugh. "Well, I don't think it would be wise to disclose all of my transgressions out in public. Let's just say his exporting business came in very handy."

"And how does Sneed fit into that?"

"Well, he was there at D'Amonico's side when the transaction took place."

"Is that so?"

Sharma nodded. "Indeed. I figured this would be very interesting to you."

"It is."

"So our talk here has been useful, then?"

"Yeah. I guess it has."

Sharma smirked. "I'm glad we made the arrangements, then. I will be waiting on that favor at some point?"

"As long as the information checks out."

"I know it will."

With having nothing else to discuss, Recker and Sharma said their goodbyes, with an understanding they'd be in touch again with each other at some point. As Recker walked away, he tapped his earpiece.

"Did you get all that?"

"Yeah," Haley replied. "I'm kind of surprised, to be honest."

"So am I."

"I felt for sure that D'Amonico was in the clear."

"Me too. Guess he threw us both for a loop."

"What now?"

"I think it's time for us to pay D'Amonico another visit. Maybe one he won't be able to talk his way out of."

20

By the time Recker and Haley would reach D'Amonico's business again, it would likely be too late, and he'd have gone home for the day. So instead of running around, they just drove straight to D'Amonico's home. Once they arrived there, they saw several cars in the circular brick driveway.

"Nice house," Haley said, looking up at it.

"Yeah. That's what you get when you skirt the rules all those years. Hefty payday."

They walked to the door and hit the button for the doorbell. Within a few seconds, the door swung open, with D'Amonico standing there. His mouth was open, stunned that he was seeing the two men again. Especially so quickly. He thought for sure he'd never see them again. He closed the door halfway, then looked behind him to make sure his wife wasn't nearby.

"What are you doing here?"

"We came to have another chat," Recker answered.

"Why? I thought everything was settled. There's nothing more to talk about."

"See, that's where you're wrong."

Then they heard Mrs. D'Amonico's voice. "Honey, who's at the door?"

"Oh, nobody, hon," D'Amonico replied. "Just a potential client. I'll take it outside."

D'Amonico rushed out the door and closed it. "You guys can't be here. I mean, really. I told you everything I know. There's nothing more to say. And the more you're here, the more you can mess things up for me. So I've been very accommodating up to this point, but now, I have to insist that you go."

"Sounds like you're a little worried about something."

"Yes, I'm worried my family is going to think I'm up to old tricks or something. I already explained that. I'm not going through that again."

"Maybe Sharma was right," Haley said.

A confused look came over D'Amonico's face. It was clear the name was familiar to him. "Sharma? Kavi Sharma?"

"That's right."

"What's he got to do with this?"

"We've heard some interesting things about your relationship with him. And with Sneed."

D'Amonico looked even more confused than before. "Who?"

"Stephen Sneed," Recker replied. "You gonna tell us you don't know him?"

D'Amonico had that look about him where there was a foul smell nearby. "What's his name?"

"Stephen Sneed."

"I don't know him. I don't think I've ever even heard the name before."

"That's not what we've been told."

"Let me guess. I can put two and two together. That idiot Sharma told you I knew him?"

Recker and Haley glanced at each other, thinking things were about to get explosive.

"Now let me take a guess," Recker said. "You're gonna deny it?"

"That's right. I don't know who this Sneed character is. Never heard of him. And if Sharma's telling you I do, he's lying to you. Flat-out lying. And that's all there is to it."

"Why would he do that?"

"Because he's a used car salesman. I mean, nothing against anyone who does that for a living or anything. But he'll sell you a lemon while telling you it's a Rolls-Royce and smile while doing it."

"Sounds like you got a history together."

D'Amonico put his hands up as if to stop himself from getting too agitated. "Look, Sharma and I did some deals back in the day. Way back in the day. Over a year or two ago."

"That's way back."

"He came to me a few months ago, looking to do another deal, and I refused. I told him I was out of the game. And he kind of blew up at me."

"What kind of deal?"

D'Amonico shrugged. "I don't know. We really didn't even get into it. He said he had some things lined up, he wanted to get them out of the country, and wanted to see if I could help. But we didn't really get into what those things were because I immediately shot him down. I told him I was out of that business and was strictly legit now. He tried to argue and say how much money was at stake, yadda, yadda, yadda, and then when I refused again, he cursed me out and hung up."

"And then what?"

"And then nothing. That was the last I've heard from him."

"And he didn't say what the deal was?"

"Just said it was a lot of money. That's it."

"What about Sneed?" Haley asked.

"I don't even know who that is."

Recker took out his phone and scrolled to Sneed's picture. He showed it to D'Amonico.

"Never seen him before."

"Sharma said he did business with you a few weeks ago," Recker said. "And Sneed was by your side. Why would he say that if it wasn't true?"

"Because if you know Kavi Sharma, he'll say

anything to deflect the heat off himself. That's who he is."

Recker happened to turn his head towards the street, which was still a good distance away. There was plenty of front acreage on the property. It wasn't like a normal house, where the street was just two or three car lengths away. In this instance, the street was about twenty or thirty yards away.

But Recker saw a slow-moving car come down the street. Its lack of speed caught his attention. Nobody drove that way, well under the speed limit, unless they were lost or had a specific reason for doing so. And considering they were there talking to D'Amonico, it made him suspicious.

Recker put his hand on D'Amonico's arm. "Get inside."

"What? Why? What's going on?"

"Nothing. Just get inside."

D'Amonico hurried inside and locked the door. Haley noticed his partner looking at the street and turned in that direction himself. He also saw the car.

"Who do you think that is?"

"Don't know," Recker replied. "Someone who has an interest in what we're doing, that's for sure."

"Who'd know we're here?"

It didn't take Recker long to think about it. There was only one name that jumped to the front of his mind.

"Kavi Sharma. He's the one that just talked to us.

He threw out D'Amonico's name. Why? He figured we'd show up here right after."

"Could be it's someone who's following D'Amonico on their own."

"If that's the case, why weren't they here already? They're just rolling up now."

"True."

"And if D'Amonico's playing it straight, and he really is legit these days, what reason would anyone have to follow him?"

"He could still be lying to us," Haley answered.

"Could be. Somebody's lying to us. But my money isn't on him."

"Sharma?"

Recker nodded. "That's who's on my betting slip."

By this time, the car was no longer moving and pulled over to the side of the road. Now it was just sitting there. Watching.

"Can you see how many are in there?" Haley asked.

"Not really."

"How do you wanna do this?"

"Well, if we start marching over there, I'm sure they'll take off long before we get there."

"Make a run for it?"

"Running's not quite what I had in mind."

21

Before the pair started walking to their car, Recker's phone rang. He answered it, not taking his eyes off the vehicle across the street for a second. He barely even glanced at the ID of who it was.

"Are you still at D'Amonico's?" Jones asked.

"Yeah. But we're leaving soon."

"I think we're barking up the wrong tree there. You should get back to the office. I have uncovered something very interesting to show you."

"All right, we'll be there soon."

Jones thought he detected a problem. It was in Recker's voice. He was very monotone. Like something else was on his mind and he was barely giving what he said a second thought. It was noticeable.

"Is something wrong?" Recker didn't answer at first. "Michael?"

"Huh?"

"I can tell something is going on. What's happening?"

"We're at D'Amonico's house. And a car just pulled up across the street."

"I'm assuming that's bad?"

"We're getting the impression that it is."

"Who's inside?"

"Can't tell," Recker answered.

"Any chance they're not there for you?"

"There's always a chance."

"But not likely?"

"Not in my mind. What's this big scoop you've got?"

"It's about Sneed," Jones replied. "I can't find any link between him and D'Amonico. But I have found one between him and Vervaat. You were right. The link is there."

"Good to know."

"That's not all."

"Oh? There's more?"

"Yes. Plenty. A powder keg. But I'll tell you when you get back here. Assuming you can lose those guys in the car."

"No worries about that," Recker said. "We'll lose them. One way or another."

"It's the 'another' part that concerns me."

"No need to. It'll be fine."

Recker hung up and put the phone back in his pocket. "David says he found a link between Sneed and Vervaat."

"Looks like we had it pegged."

"Says there's more, but will tell us when we get back to the office."

"What do you wanna do with these guys?"

Recker grinned. "Let's take them on a little ride."

"And do what with them?"

"Well, we'll see how they wanna play it. If they want to be cooperative, we might get a few more answers out of them than we had before."

"And if they're not feeling so cooperative?" Haley asked.

"Then I guess they'll go the same route Sneed and his friends did."

Recker and Haley casually walked back to their car and got in. Since they were a good distance away, they weren't worried about being fired upon yet. Once they pulled out of the driveway and started driving down the road, they looked in the mirrors to see if they were being followed. They were.

"I don't understand what Sharma's doing," Haley said. "If these are his guys, why would he jeopardize what he just agreed to? He could've gotten a favor somewhere down the line. Wouldn't that be more valuable than checking up on us and whatever we're doing?"

"I think it's pretty obvious by now that it was all a sham. He had nothing for us. I think he was just hoping to find out what we knew. And then throw us off the track."

"Throw us off the track? That would imply that he's in on everything. Otherwise there'd be no need."

Recker couldn't dispute the point. "Even if we don't understand the how's or why's yet, we can't ignore the proof that's staring us in the face."

Considering they knew they weren't followed, and if they went under the assumption that D'Amonico was legit these days, Sharma being behind this was the only thing that made sense at the moment. Nobody else would have known they were there. The only other possibility was that D'Amonico had some guards on the lookout. But that was dismissed quickly. If D'Amonico had guards, why weren't they at his place of business when he was there too. And they never saw one at the party they attended either. It didn't make sense.

But Sharma did make sense. They already identified him as a manipulative kind of guy. And they just did leave him. And he was the only one who knew they were heading to D'Amonico's. All the pieces fit the puzzle.

The only wildcard in their thinking was if the people in that car were there for D'Amonico for some reason. But if he was clean, there'd be no reason to do so. That would also mean spotting the car, and them showing up there to begin with, was some kind of coincidence. And as everyone knew, Recker didn't put much stock into those.

All roads led back to Sharma. Plus the fact that the

car was following them, it didn't leave much room for doubt. With Haley behind the wheel, he was driving without a clear destination in mind.

"How far out do you wanna take this?"

"Let's go somewhere secluded," Recker replied. "If it gets hairy, no use in getting other people involved. Or have there be witnesses."

"I got an idea. Don't know how you'll feel about it."

"Go ahead and say it."

"How about if we see if Vincent can lend us the use of one of his properties? Familiar territory. And we won't have to worry about eyes that shouldn't be there."

Recker thought it over for a minute. He came around to that line of thinking.

"I like it. I'll call Malloy and see if there's something we can use."

Recker instantly dialed Malloy's number. Thankfully, he picked up right away. If he didn't, it wouldn't have been a big deal, as they would've thought of something else. But this did seem the easier way.

"Hey, what's up?"

"Kind of have a problem right now," Recker answered. "Not a big problem. Not an urgent problem. But if you could lend me a hand, I'd sure appreciate it."

"Sure. What do you need?"

"Just the use of a property somewhere. Preferably secluded and no foot traffic."

Malloy instantly knew where this conversation was headed. "Is this going to require a cleanup?"

"Quite possible. If it does, we'll handle it. If it's not possible, or is too complicated on a short notice, it's no problem. We can figure out another option."

"Nah, nah, it's fine. I got something for you. Take them down to the Blue. You know the one."

"By the river?"

"Yeah. It's empty right now."

"Isn't there a gate?"

"I'll have someone go unlock it," Malloy replied. "Nobody's there. Should suit your needs. How far away from it are you?"

Recker quickly typed in the address. The property, mostly called Blue by Vincent's men, because of its blue roof, was well known to Recker and Haley. They'd been there several times before. It was mostly used as a storage place for Vincent. Both crates of product, and vehicles, were stashed around there.

"Looks like about thirty minutes," Recker said.

"I'll have it open for you," Malloy replied.

"Thanks. I appreciate it."

"Need any help?"

"No, I think we got it. Just one car behind us. Just two men that I can tell. Should be good. If things get dicey, just didn't want to be dropping bodies on the street."

"I hear that. If things change, let me know."

"Will do."

"Good to go?" Haley asked.

"Good to go. Head to the Blue."

"Should be a good spot."

"Yeah, should be. He said nobody's there right now. He'll make sure the gate's open for us when we get there."

"What do you wanna do when we get there? Block them in, hope we can get them to surrender? Get them to talk? Or just blast away?"

"Let's try the easier way first," Recker answered. "If we can get them to see they're fighting a losing cause, maybe they'll be more receptive to talking. Then we can get the answers we need to wrap this thing up."

"Who knows? Maybe they'll eagerly throw their hands up and jump into our arms."

Recker laughed. "Yeah. Wouldn't that be nice? Somehow, I don't think we'll be that lucky."

22

———

When Recker and Haley arrived at the Blue building, they found the front gate unlocked, and opened, just like it was promised. They didn't bother to stop, at least not on the outside. But there was a small bit of distance between them and the following car. Not a big distance, but large enough for Haley to slow the car down once they were inside the property. Without stopping, though the car was only going a few miles per hour, Recker opened his door and jumped out.

With Recker out of the car, Haley kept on going. Recker quickly took up a spot behind a nearby car that was parked, and ducked behind it. As the pursuing car drove through, Recker hurried over to the gate and closed it.

Within a minute or two, Haley had returned. He drove around the Blue building, and then made his way back to the front gate, parking in front of it. Seconds later, they saw the other car making its way to them. It stopped about halfway between the building and the gate. With the gate locked, and the car parked in front of it, the men knew they were now in a jam.

Both Recker and Haley were out of the car, standing behind it as they waited for the other men to make the first move. They stood there for a couple of minutes, as it appeared like the other men were considering all their options. But they didn't have many. There was only one way out of there. Vincent made sure of that when they made alterations to the place. One entrance, high fences, no way to escape other than the way they came in.

Finally, after several minutes of silence, and waiting, the doors to the other car opened up. Though Recker and Haley couldn't initially tell how many men were in the car following them, it was now easy. All four doors opened up.

"They must've been scrunched down on the floor," Haley said.

Recker smirked, thinking it was amusing, though he didn't have a comeback. He was focused completely on the men in front of him.

"Looks like you guys are lost," Recker said.

The driver shook his head. "Nope."

Recker could tell this was not going to go down the way he hoped. The way he expected, sure, but not the way he hoped. He could see several of the men had guns sticking out of their pants. That wasn't accidental. He was sure they'd be reaching for them soon enough.

"Why don't you guys drop your guns and we can talk about things."

"I don't think so," the driver replied.

"This doesn't have to end badly for anyone."

The driver looked around at his friends. He counted the odds in his favor. "The only one it's going to end badly for is you."

"Things don't have to get hostile," Recker said. "All we wanna know is what you're here for, who sent you, and once you tell us, you can be on your way."

"Or we can kill you, then be on our way anyway."

"Is that really what Sharma wants?"

Though Recker wasn't a hundred percent positive it was Sharma's men standing in front of him, he thought it was extremely likely. And what better way to find out than by tossing the man's name out there? He was sure he'd get a response.

"We're here, aren't we? That should answer your question."

"Why not?" Recker asked. "I just met with him a little while ago. Why didn't he try something then?"

"Because he's not an idiot. He knew your partner was out there watching and waiting. He does something to you, your partner does something to him. It's pretty simple. Plus, he wanted to find out what you knew exactly."

"Like all that nonsense about Sneed knowing D'Amonico?"

"I don't know about all that. But if you drop your guns, maybe you can figure a way out of this."

"I don't think that's likely," Recker said.

"Which part?"

"Either."

"Well, we'll tell Sharma that this is the way you wanted it."

"I don't think you're gonna be breathing long enough to tell him anything."

The driver instantly reached for his gun, but Recker blasted a hole through his chest before he was able to pull his pistol. Haley then took care of the guy on the passenger side. The two remaining men retreated to the bumper and crouched down.

For the next minute or two, nobody was firing. They seemed to be at a stalemate. Recker and Haley didn't feel the need to change positions and risk exposing themselves, especially when there was only one way out and they were blocking it. And the two men behind the other car didn't feel like sticking their heads out and risk having them blown off.

Eventually, something would have to give. After another minute or two, the men behind the car began getting nervous and started firing wildly. None of the shots were close to hitting their targets. Recker and Haley were still staying patient. Waiting for one of the men to get overanxious and expose themselves.

The standoff didn't last much longer, though. Five more minutes went by and more shots were fired. But these ones sounded different. They weren't fired by Recker or Haley. And it didn't sound the same as the ones that Sharma's men had previously fired.

Recker peeked around the edge of their car and saw two more bodies lying on the ground than were there previously. The two men at the rear bumper were now dead. Blood was staining the surrounding ground. Recker and Haley stayed down, not sure what was happening, readying themselves for another fight if need be.

Then they heard another voice. This one was familiar.

"Mike! Chris! I'm coming in!"

Recker and Haley glanced at each other, surprised at the voice they were hearing. Knowing everything was handled, and it was safe to show themselves, they both stood up. They walked around the car and saw Malloy walking towards them from the back of the property. He had two of his men behind him. Recker and Haley also started walking, and they met near the car of Sharma's men.

Malloy smiled at them. "How's it going?"

Recker crossed his arms, not sure what was happening. He wasn't mad, just confused. "You wanna tell me what you're doing here?"

"Well, you didn't figure I was going to let you have all the fun for yourself, did you?"

"How'd you get here? Were you hiding in here? There's only one entrance."

Malloy closed his eyes, turned his head, and scratched his neck. "Wellll, that's not exactly true. There's another way in here. Hidden in case of emergencies. You know how it is. You didn't think we'd allow ourselves to get boxed in here if something ever happened, did you?"

"No, I suppose not."

"Good thing we were here, too. Looked like you needed the help."

"We would've handled it," Recker said.

"Oh, I'm sure, I'm sure. We just moved it along a bit."

"Why bother?"

Malloy shrugged. "Well, it is our property. I just figured one of us should be here for the festivities." He then looked down at the bodies. "Who are these guys, anyway?"

"I believe they work for Kavi Sharma."

"Sharma? That crumb? Good riddance."

"What do you know about him?"

"Ah, not much," Malloy answered. "He's just one of those little weasels that come out of the woodwork whenever they smell something, you know? Spineless. What's he after you for?"

"Guess we're stepping on some toes."

"You must've made them hurt if he's pulling this on you. Not exactly what he's known for. I mean, sure, he'll use muscle when he has to, but it's not his strength. Sure not his strength now that he's got four men lying here."

"How many more's he got, you figure?"

"Tough to say. Never heard an exact figure on it. I'd say..." he took another look at the bodies. "Well now I'd say around ten to fifteen. Could be less. He's not a major player. He wants to be. But he's not there yet."

"Well... I'm about to make sure he never gets there."

23

Malloy agreed to take care of the bodies left at the Blue building. Since he killed two of them, and it was on Vincent's property, he thought it was only fair. Plus, he knew Recker had more important matters to take care of.

Recker and Haley went back to the office, where they met Jones in his usual position. They went right over to him, knowing he had some information for them.

"What's the big powder keg you got?" Recker asked, not wanting to waste any time.

"Before we get into that, I ran the four men you just eliminated from the world of breathing through our software programs."

"And?"

"I have established a link to Sharma," Jones

answered. "At least for two of them. Not yet with the other two."

"Stands to reason that the others do too," Haley replied.

"Yes, I agree. And with the two of them, it's overwhelming evidence. There is no doubt of their connection."

Though it was nice to hear it confirmed, Recker was still more interested in the link between Sneed and Vervaat.

"What about the connection to Vervaat?"

"First off, I did some more checking on whether I could find some link between Sneed and D'Amonico. I could not find any."

"Vervaat?" Recker impatiently asked.

"Yes, yes, the connection between Sneed and Vervaat is real and verified."

"So what is it?"

"It goes back some years," Jones replied.

"Are you gonna tell me they went to high school together or something?"

"No. There was actually an incident about ten years ago where Sneed was arrested for something. Small infraction. But guess who bailed him out?"

"Damien Vervaat?"

Jones smiled. "Bingo."

"So obviously Sneed was working for him at that time too," Haley said.

"Most likely."

"So whatever happened, he's probably been working for Vervaat ever since."

"I would assume so. Which also means that whatever Sharma told you about Sneed being with D'Amonico is likely garbage."

"Already assumed as much," Recker said.

"Sharma was deliberately trying to throw us off Vervaat's trail," Haley said. "There's only one reason for that."

"Two."

"He knows exactly what's going on with these diamond robberies. What's the second?"

"He's probably in on it," Recker said. "Why else bother?"

"Unless he's getting some kind of hush money out of it?"

"That still puts him in the middle of it, regardless."

"Yeah, I guess it does."

"Either way, Sharma and Vervaat are in this thing together. Either directly or indirectly. Doesn't really matter which. They're both going down now."

Jones threw his hands up, as if he were being shunned. "I have more, you know."

"Oh, you do?"

"Yes, I do."

"The powder keg?"

"I thought that was it," Recker said.

"Really?"

Recker shrugged. "Sorry."

"The powder keg is that I have also already established a connection between Vervaat and Sharma."

"Really?"

"Yes, really. Stop sounding so surprised. I am good at this, you know."

"Yeah, I know, but I was just, uh... ah, nevermind. What did you find?"

"A transaction," Jones answered. "Actually, several of them. It took some digging on this, going through multiple banking transactions. They tried to hide it, going through different banks and whatnot, but I have clearly established a connection between all of them, eventually tying them back to accounts owned by Vervaat, and Sharma."

Jones shuffled some papers around on his desk before finding the ones he needed. He then handed the copies over to both Recker and Haley so they could take a look. There were a lot of numbers on there, complete with red marks, circles, and arrows, alerting them to the points of interest. Recker and Haley read everything, though it was a little confusing by itself. Still, they were sure Jones had it worked out completely. And accurately.

"You're sure about all this?" Recker asked.

Jones rolled his eyes. "Am I sure? Really? Of course I'm sure. I wouldn't have mentioned it to you if I wasn't. You know I am very thorough in everything I do."

Recker smiled. "Just making sure. All of us are fallible every now and again."

"There is no doubt. Their accounts are linked on twelve different transactions going back two years. And look at the date on the latest transaction."

Recker shuffled the papers around to get to it. "A week after the first diamond robbery."

"Ten thousand dollars."

"Half the amount of the value."

Jones nodded, a satisfying look on his face, pleased with the work that he'd done.

"So much for Sharma only taking on big jobs and not worrying about the small stuff," Haley said.

"Obviously he was just saying that to throw you off the tracks," Jones replied.

"Obviously."

"It does raise the point of why he'd bother going through with this charade to begin with, though."

"That's pretty easy to understand, actually," Recker said.

"Why?"

"Don't forget, we rolled up on him in a hurry. We surprised him. We were an unexpected complication. He wasn't planning on us."

"So he panicked?"

"Probably at first. Then he thought he could use us to his advantage. He tried to play it off like he could help us get what we want."

"All while hiding himself."

"That's right," Recker said. "So he tells us he wouldn't bother with small jobs, he throws out Sneed's name, tells us about D'Amonico, all while he's sliding under the radar."

"So he gets away with it while his competition gets eliminated."

"I don't know if it's competition. D'Amonico's not involved in anything anymore. I think it's more getting us further away from him, and that he's mad at D'Amonico for not helping him out to begin with."

"Whatever the thing is, it didn't work," Haley said. "Now he's got a target on his chest."

Recker nodded. "And it's center mass."

Recker went over to the drawer and pulled out the phone that he'd been using to communicate with Sharma. His actions drew a look from one of his partners, unsure of what he was planning.

"What are you doing?" Jones asked.

"Going to talk to our friend."

"Why would you want to do that?"

"See what he's thinking," Recker answered.

"No, no, no. I don't see what that will accomplish. Everyone now knows exactly what's going on."

"Yeah, but does he know he's got four men down?"

"Well I'm sure he does by now!"

"Maybe. I just want him to know I'm coming."

"I'm sure he knows. I don't think broadcasting it helps much."

Recker smiled. "Yeah, but... I still want him to know I'm coming."

Jones shook his head, knowing his pleas were falling on deaf ears. He'd seen this movie play out too many times. Recker dialed the number he had for Sharma. He actually didn't think the man would pick up. To his surprise, Sharma answered.

"Hello there."

"Hello yourself," Recker said.

"I'm sure of the reason you're calling and I want to explain what happened to avoid any misunderstandings."

"Oh, OK. You do that."

"I understand you had an altercation with my men."

"I guess you could call it that."

"And they're no longer among the living, right?"

"That's correct," Recker replied.

"Most unfortunate. I'm sure you are probably livid in thinking they were there for you."

"Crossed my mind."

"Let me assure you this is not the case. After you left, their orders were to go to D'Amonico's house and lean on him. That is all. They were not there for you. I want to make sure there are no misunderstandings."

"Oh, there are no misunderstandings."

"Good. I do not want there to be any hard feelings between us. I hold you in the highest regard."

"I can see that," Recker said.

"If there's anything else you need, feel free to ask."

Recker chuckled. Man, this guy was something else, he thought. Sharma had a master's degree in BS. Bullshit. And he was good at it. There was no doubt about that. The man could talk. But there was never anything of substance. That much was clear.

"Are you done?"

"Excuse me?" Sharma said.

"Are you done lying out of both sides of your mouth?"

"I assure you..."

"No, I don't wanna hear anymore of your nonsense. I'm gonna tell you. So shut up and listen."

Sharma didn't let out a peep.

"I know those guys were there for us. They told us that before they were taken out. We also know about the link between you and Vervaat. And the link between Sneed and Vervaat. So everything is starting to add up. Including your involvement. Like the ten thousand dollars you got after the first diamond robbery."

"Let me explain..."

"No, there's no explaining to do. There's nothing you can say. We know you're involved. And you're not going to weasel your way out of it."

"There must be..."

Recker wasn't going to let him get a word in. "I told you when we first met that I didn't have time for games."

"I remember that clearly."

"Obviously it didn't sink in. So let this sink in. I'm coming for you. Just like I told you I would. I told you that if you lie to me, and I find out you're involved, that I'd be your worst nightmare. And I will be. So don't close your eyes. Because I'm a nightmare you won't wake up from."

24

Recker and Haley got ready to leave the office, though it really didn't take much. They were already pretty worked up from the day's events. They just had to grab some ammo.

"Do you really think that was a good idea?" Jones asked.

"Why not?"

"You basically just sent out a nationwide broadcast that you were coming for him."

"He already knew I was coming for him," Recker replied. "Once he found out his men were dead, that sealed the deal. That was the mashed potatoes. What I told him was the gravy."

"I'm not sure how the food metaphor works, but... I still think it would have been better to move in more quietly."

"Now he's worried. I guarantee he doesn't have the

stomach for what's coming. He's gonna panic, make a mistake, do something to our advantage."

"Sure about that?"

Recker smiled. "Reasonably."

"Or, you know, you could've tried to surprise him. Not give him time to react. Showed up at his doorstep suddenly, as it were."

"Nah. Where's the fun in that?"

"Fun. Yes. Well."

"I hear what you're saying," Recker said. "But he knew this was coming the minute he told those guys to follow us. We weren't going to surprise him no matter what."

"We will just have to disagree on that point. Plus, you're already an hour away from him."

Recker and Haley headed for the door, but stopped just short of it when they heard one of the alerts go off on one of the computers. They turned around and waited for Jones to inform them of what was going on.

"I've been monitoring Sharma's text messages."

"And?" Recker said.

"He just sent a message to, I assume one of his men, telling him to meet him at..." Jones then wrote down the address on a piece of paper and handed it to his partners. "This address."

"Where's this?"

Jones typed in the address and saw that it was some type of office/warehouse building. It didn't look to be a large building. One floor. And it wasn't connected to anything else. Another alert went off and Jones' eyes went to the computer.

"Sharma just said he's going to attempt to have you meet him there."

"Really?" Recker said, slightly surprised. "Under the guise of a meeting. He's going to ask you to come talk, try to smooth things over, while he's really going to ambush you."

Recker laughed. "That's what I like. Predictability."

"Wonder when this call's going to come in?" Haley asked.

"Might take some time. He's gonna want to put some things in place first."

"Maybe not. What if he puts everything together and you don't show up? Then he did it all for nothing."

"That's true."

"I'd think he's going to want to make sure you're confirmed before moving his chess pieces around."

"Yeah, maybe."

Recker grabbed the prepaid phone and took it with him, assuming he was going to get a call at some point. It came a lot sooner than he expected, though. Recker and Haley barely made it to their car in the parking lot before it rang. But Recker didn't answer it.

"Let him sweat it out a bit first."

"It'll give us some extra time anyway," Haley said. "The building's about forty-five minutes from here."

"Yeah. I want to try and get as close to it as possible

before confirming we're showing up. We can catch them off guard that way."

"Sure would be nice to know how many we're going up against."

"Malloy didn't put them at more than ten or fifteen," Recker said.

"Yeah, but how old's that information?"

Haley got behind the wheel and pulled out onto the road. As they drove, another phone call came in. Recker didn't answer that one either.

"I'll give it another ten minutes," Recker said.

It was almost ten minutes exactly when Sharma tried again. This time, Recker picked up.

"What's so important that you're blowing my phone up?"

"I am just trying to make amends," Sharma replied. "I realize things have gotten off on the wrong foot here, and I want to have the chance to make it up to you."

"Yeah? How do you think you can do that?"

"Come meet me. I have all the evidence you need to put this case behind you. I can wrap everything in a bow for you. The diamonds, Vervaat, everything."

"And what do you get out of it?"

"The chance to slip into the background?"

"You want to skate free and clear from this?" Recker asked. "That's what you want?"

"Yes. I am not at the forefront of this. I just want to back away and you can do what you want with the others."

"What makes you think I'll believe you?"

"Because I wouldn't be making this call otherwise. I'd be on a plane somewhere already. I am trying to make it right."

"So what do you have?"

"Come meet me and I will show you," Sharma answered. "It's all on documents and emails and things. I will print everything out and put it in a folder for you."

"Meet you where?"

"2398 West Benson Drive."

"And your guards?"

"It will just be me. You can even bring your friend if you like. No tricks. I give you my word."

Recker smiled. He knew what that was worth. Still, it was going as he predicted it would. And he was willing to play along.

"OK, fine. I'll meet you there. But it's just going to be me."

"Anything you want," Sharma replied.

"But I'll give you another warning. If I see anyone else, a guard, a janitor, someone painting the side of the building, I don't care who, I'm coming up shooting. Do you understand?"

"Perfectly. I assure you there will be no tricks, and there will be no other people around. I will be waiting in my office for you to arrive."

"And where is that?" Recker asked.

"The office and warehouse are attached to each

other. The office is the smaller building to the left. Go inside, it will be unlocked, go to your left and down a small hallway. I will be inside my office on the left-hand side waiting for you."

"With no tricks?"

"No tricks. I give you my word."

"So you've said."

"As I've said, I only want to make things right. I'll give you everything you need."

"All right," Recker said. "I'll be there."

"Great. I look forward to your arrival and putting this unfortunate mess behind us. How soon can you be here?"

Recker glanced at the time. They should get there in about fifteen minutes.

"Give me about an hour. I'm just finishing up something first."

"As you wish. No problem. One hour. I'll be waiting."

Recker hung up. "Yeah. I'm sure you will be."

25

Recker and Haley arrived at the building next to the one Sharma was referencing. They were very early and had some time to prepare. The two buildings had a line of Emerald Green Arborvitae trees between them, about fifteen feet high, so Sharma wouldn't be able to notice that they were there already.

The parking lot they were in was fairly packed, as it seemed to be some kind of industrial plant. It would help them to blend in. Between the cars and the trees, they wouldn't be seen. Recker and Haley both got out of the car and moved around to the back of the industrial building. The trees disguised their movements.

There was some thought about Haley going in by himself and waiting until Recker showed up in the car, and then they'd start picking everyone off. But then they figured they would be putting themselves at a disadvantage. Right now, they had the element of surprise. They weren't expected for at least another half an hour. It was time they could use.

Recker and Haley stood near the edge of the trees, staring at the back of Sharma's building. They could see several cameras mounted at the top of it.

"That might be problematic," Haley said.

They didn't see any cars in front, though they would have been more surprised if they did. Sharma wouldn't have advertised that more men were there than what was supposed to be.

"We might've beaten them here."

It was possible, Recker thought. But he wasn't sure he'd put any money on it. Even though Recker delayed taking the call and confirming he was coming, it was still a long drive from when Jones first intercepted the message Sharma sent his cronies. There was enough time between then and now to get there and set things up.

Recker wasn't willing to bet that nobody was inside monitoring the cameras. But he was looking for blind spots. Many security systems had them. Though he didn't see any at first here. There seemed to be one at the back door to both the office area and the warehouse.

"We're gonna have to take a chance somewhere," Haley said.

Recker agreed, but he didn't want to just advertise their presence so easily. He then studied the side of the building a little more closely. There were cameras stationed in the middle of it, near the top. But both cameras were pointing towards the edges of the building on each side. It looked like that left the middle part exposed.

"What about there?" Recker asked, pointing to a window in the middle, directly under the cameras.

"Except we don't know where that leads."

"Well, we don't know where anything else leads exactly either."

"True. What if it's directly to Sharma's office?"

Recker snickered. "Then I guess he'll get a surprise, won't he?"

"Looks like it might be our best option. Let's hit it."

With it being their best, and maybe only option, they started moving in that direction. They moved beyond the Arborvitae's, now out of view from the industrial plant, though they stayed close to the trees, almost hugging them. Though the cameras weren't pointed at them, they weren't sure how far laterally it would pick up. So they had to move in at just the right time.

Once they had gotten to right across from the window, they made their move. They scurried over to the window, directly underneath the cameras. They were assuming they weren't picked up by the cameras, though they couldn't be sure. Still, this was their best play, regardless.

The window wasn't big, but it was big enough for a body to crawl through. They couldn't see inside yet, as there were some blinds that were down on the other side of it.

"I don't suppose you brought your window-cracking tools," Haley joked.

"Left them with my door-breaking equipment."

"Figured as much. Guess we'll have to do it the old-fashioned way."

"I'll cover you," Recker said. "Try not to make it too loud."

Recker had his gun out and alternated looking at both sides of the building, while waiting for his partner to get themselves inside. It wouldn't take long. With no better options, Haley just took his gun and smashed a small piece of the window out. Towards the bottom so he could unlock the window.

"Hope nobody's inside to hear that," Haley said.

He stuck his fingers through the broken glass, and peeked through the blinds to see if someone was on the other side. They didn't want to go in there if there was already someone waiting for them.

"Looks clear."

Recker continued providing cover, as his partner stuck his hand through the window and unlocked it. He then pushed it up. Haley pushed the blinds up and stuck his head under them, just to take another look inside. It looked like some sort of office, though there was no one in there. He quickly found the strings to the blinds and pulled them up fully.

"We're good."

Haley went in first. As soon as he was inside, then Recker crawled through. With both of them inside, they closed the window again, and put down the blinds. If anybody walked around the property, they didn't want them to see an open window and blinds that weren't there. That'd be a dead giveaway someone had broken in. Of course, there was the fact that the window was broken, but they'd just have to hope that nobody noticed.

As Recker's eyes darted around the office, Haley was over by the door. His ear was right on it.

"I hear voices," Haley whispered.

"How many?"

"Tough to tell. Three? Maybe four?"

"Sharma?"

"Can't tell."

Haley then put his arm up. "Wait. Sounds like more coming."

Recker went over to the door himself, also putting his ear up to it. It sounded like the men were in the hallway, not too far from the office. They appeared to be putting some plans together. They listened for about a minute. It sounded like the men were disagreeing about where they wanted to set up. A couple voices were raised. Recker thought this could have been a golden opportunity. They couldn't be sure how many were out there, but it didn't really matter. They'd never suspect what was coming.

Recker motioned with his hands to his partner

what he wanted to do. They'd throw open the door, then they'd each take a separate direction. Recker would spin to the right, while Haley would take to the left. They'd start throwing bullets as soon as they jumped into the hallway. Sharma's men wouldn't know what hit them.

Recker gave his partner one final glance before he threw open the door.

"You ready?"

Haley nodded. "Let's start the party."

26

Recker took one final huff, then flung open the door. He jumped into the hallway and immediately faced to his right. There were four men standing there. They had no idea what was coming. Haley was right behind his partner and maneuvered to his left. There were three of Sharma's men on that side.

On each side, the men were blissfully unaware of what was waiting for them. A couple of them were leaning up against the wall. A couple others had hands in their pockets. And two others were consumed by their cigarettes. None of them were in any position to fight back.

They tried, though. As soon as they saw the two intruders jump into the hallway, all of them reached for their guns. They just weren't fast enough. Not with the kind of advantage Recker and Haley had.

Only two of them were actually able to bring their

weapons out in front of them as if they were about to fire. But they weren't even able to get shots off. In a matter of a short few seconds, all eight men were down. And they weren't getting back up. Not at that range.

Recker and Haley briefly looked down at their handiwork, then braced themselves in case there were more coming. Especially if they heard the fireworks. Nobody else was on the horizon yet, though. The two partners looked at each other for a moment.

"Not bad," Recker said.

"You don't suppose we were lucky enough to get them all in one shot, do you?"

Recker grinned, wishing the thought were true, though he knew it wasn't. "Not likely. The big dog isn't here."

"What if he's not even here? What if he sent these guys to do the dirty work?"

Recker grimaced. "No, I don't think so. I think he'd have to make an appearance for this to work. If I didn't see him, I'd immediately have my guard up. That's what he was trying to prevent. He was hoping for something easy."

The two of them then checked the rest of the offices that were nearby. They were hoping they'd find Sharma in one of them. They did find the one that appeared to be his, though he wasn't inside. There were a few pictures of him on the wall and on the desk.

"Where do you think the rest are?"

"We haven't tried the warehouse yet," Recker answered.

They walked around the corner, which led to another door, which was the inside entrance to the warehouse area.

"If they're in there, they heard what happened," Haley said. "And they're probably waiting for us."

"Probably."

It was a solid door, so they couldn't see through it to see what was waiting for them, if anything. But they didn't exactly get good vibes as they waited there. Haley stood there for a minute, while Recker went back to the front of the building and looked out one of the windows that overlooked the parking area. There were no cars there. He reported back to his partner.

"No cars."

"So how'd these guys get here?" Haley said.

"Either got dropped off, or their cars are in that warehouse."

"And there could be more."

Recker nodded. "Could be."

"Go in guns blazing?"

"I'd rather not. They could have someone with a shotgun pointed right at that door when we open it. Plus, they're expecting us to go through this door."

"Go around the other side?"

"How about you go around to the back door? If I hear gunfire, they'll be distracted towards you. That'll give me an opportunity to come in through here."

"If we got numbers right, there should be no more than what... six or eight?"

"Something like that."

Haley tapped his partner on the arm as he left him. "See you in a few."

Recker waited by the door, next to it in case someone on the other side decided to start blindly blasting away. Haley ran out the back door to the office area. Now outside again, he wasn't concerned about the cameras anymore. They were hooked up to a bunch of computers in one of the other offices they checked. So now they knew they weren't being watched.

Haley went down to the other end of the building to where the warehouse was. There was a steel door waiting for him. He took a few deep breaths, then put his hand on it and yanked the door open. He then ducked to the side as he did.

He was right to feel iffy about it, because as soon as he pulled it open, gunfire erupted. The door was sprayed with bullets. As soon as Recker heard that, he threw open his door, as well. He tried a different tactic, though. Instead of standing there, looking for a target, or barging right in, he dropped to the ground.

Bullets flew over his head as Recker crawled in. There were some boxes and shelves to the right side. But there was a lot of emptiness ahead of him. Along with some cars that were parked, as he suspected there would be. Quickly scanning the area, he found the shooter that was stationed there. Well, he saw the man's legs. The rest of him was concealed by some wire shelving he was standing behind. There were boxes on most of the shelves to block his appearance.

But there was no hiding his legs. Specifically, from the knees down. Recker fired four times, with three of the bullets finding the mark. The man instantly dropped to the ground and clutched at his leg.

Recker immediately jumped to his knees, then scurried around to the man's position. He was still keeping down in case anyone else in there had him in their sights. Just as Recker made his way around the shelf, the man was able to grab his gun. As soon as he saw Recker, he brought his gun up, ready to fire. Recker was just a tad faster, putting a bullet in the man before he was able to fire.

Recker looked up, still hearing loads of gunfire. In the closed quarters, it sounded like an army was firing away. He moved on from his position, looking to take out the next man he came across. And it wouldn't take long.

He looked over at one of the parked cars and saw another man standing beside it. The driver's side door was open, and the man was crouched down behind it. He was shooting in Haley's direction.

Recker wasn't crazy about the angle he had. He could've taken the shot, but he didn't want to take the chance of missing. Then the man could have returned fire, putting Recker in a vulnerable position. Recker wanted to make sure he had the perfect spot.

He took a quick look around, then saw a pallet of boxes a little to the right. While the man was busy firing at Haley, Recker hurried over to the pallet. The man never noticed him. Recker was then able to sneak up behind him.

Recker only needed one shot, though he fired an extra round just for good measure. Recker then peeked his head around the pallet, looking for another target. He still heard gunfire. He detected it was coming from around a car in the corner of the building. He was just about to make his way over there when the gunfire suddenly stopped.

It was now eerily quiet in there. A far cry from the previous few minutes when it sounded like they were in a shooting range. There wasn't a sound to be heard. Recker moved his head in every direction to see if there were any more signs of life anywhere. He couldn't find any.

A few minutes went by. These were often the most anxious moments for Recker. It wasn't when the battle first started. That was easy. You already knew what you were walking into. It was the moments when you weren't sure whether or not a battle was finished. If you guessed it was done, and you were wrong, you would quite likely walk right into a bullet with your name on it.

"Mike?"

Recker didn't respond at first to his partner, still a bit hesitant. "I'm here."

He slowly rose up, making himself a little more visible. His head was still turning in what seemed like a million directions. He saw Haley walk over to him. They both still had their guns out, ready to fire if need be. It didn't seem like it would be necessary, though.

"Looks like that's it," Haley said.

Recker took one more look around. "Yeah, looks like it."

The two of them started walking around the warehouse, checking on the bodies, just to make sure they were dead. Everyone was. There were thirteen bodies in total. Eight in the hallway, and five in the warehouse. But they were missing one. The one in charge of it all.

"Sharma's not here."

Recker shook his head. "No, he's not."

"Wonder if he got spooked first."

"Maybe. Or maybe he just didn't want to be here when the shooting started."

"It's not finished, then."

"Wasn't finished anyway," Recker said. "Still got Vervaat to worry about."

"I meant this part of it."

"Still got some work to do on that front, I guess."

"We do. But maybe not as much as we think."

"How do you mean?"

"I have a feeling that the next time we find Sharma, we'll be finding Vervaat too."

"You think they're together?"

"Why not? They've apparently been working together all this time."

"Maybe. Sure would've been nice to put a nail in his coffin here, though. Just to save us some time. And energy."

"Don't worry," Recker said. "We'll be putting a nail in his coffin soon enough."

27

By the time Recker and Haley got back to the office, they had conflicted feelings about everything that had happened so far. While it appeared that they eliminated most, if not all, of Sharma's organization, they didn't get the top guy yet. And now he might have been in the wind. But regardless of how they felt about Sharma, they had to make sure they didn't get into the trap of worrying about him and losing focus on everything else. There was still more at play here. In fact, they were just about to find out how much more.

As soon as Recker and Haley marched into the office, they could immediately tell Jones had a problem. He was shaking his head as he was typing, along with making a few noises that sounded like he was frustrated. It was a dead giveaway.

"Something wrong?" Recker asked.

Jones never broke his typing stride as he answered. "You might say that."

"Wanna share?"

"While you two were out playing The Lone Ranger, we had another situation break."

"What happened?"

"Another diamond robbery."

"What?! Already?!"

"Yes. Already."

"That doesn't fit the pattern," Haley said. "It's too soon."

"Well it appears they have broken free of that pattern."

"That's why Sharma wasn't there," Recker said. "Just another way of drawing us out. He knew we obviously wouldn't be there to stop any robbery if we were supposed to be at a meeting with him."

"And he sacrificed his men for it," Haley replied.

"I'm not so sure he sacrificed them. He might have genuinely felt like they could've taken care of us. Or maybe he was hoping for both outcomes. We're out of the way, so he knows they can pull off whatever job they have lined up, and maybe they could kill us in the process. A win-win if they could make it happen."

"Even still, one out of two isn't bad," Jones said. "Especially at the take."

"You got a total already?"

"I do. Estimated at over five hundred thousand."

Haley whistled. "Upping the stakes big-time."

"Now the question is how many more jobs do they have in them?" Recker asked.

"I'm not sure they have any."

"What makes you think that?"

"These last two jobs were a little faster than the others. To me, that means they've pulled them off faster than they wanted to. Probably because they were feeling the heat from us."

"Doesn't mean they're done."

"No, but I have a feeling they moved them up so they could finish early, or at least take an extended break. They knew they could keep us busy during these last couple times. But how many more times will they be able to do that?"

Recker nodded, seeing his partner's point. "We're obviously not going to agree to any more meetings."

"So I just have a feeling that maybe we won't hear from them for a while. Hope we get bogged down with other things, stop worrying about them. Then they'll strike. But I have a feeling it won't be for a month or two. Maybe longer."

"You could be right about that. But that means they'll be in the wind for a while."

"Not if we find them first. They haven't exactly been hiding so far."

"I have a feeling that might be changing," Recker replied. He wiped his face. "Any leads on this latest robbery?"

"Not so far," Jones answered. "Same as before.

Three men. Covered. Got into a car on the street. Stolen."

"Any pattern to all the stolen cars? Location, maybe?"

"No. All from different areas. No discernible pattern that I can tell."

"So we're no closer than we have been?"

"At the moment. We all know that can change on a dime."

"It better start raining them soon," Recker said.

"Take another crack at Vervaat's office?" Haley asked.

Recker seemed ambivalent. "I'm not sure how much good that'll do. I have a feeling he's not showing up there again."

"Or we can try his house."

Recker didn't seem excited about those prospects either. He got the feeling both Vervaat and Sharma were going to exit the public eye for a little bit. Wait for a more opportunistic time to reappear. Especially one where the Silencers weren't right on their tail.

"What other options do we have at the moment?" Haley asked.

Recker conceded. "None, really."

"Might as well give it a shot. Who knows what we might find? Maybe we don't have it pegged like we thought."

Recker finally agreed. "Yeah, worth a shot, I guess.

I'm not feeling too hopeful, but maybe I'll be surprised."

Jones kept working on the latest robbery, hoping he could find something that could tie it together with the other ones. He was hoping to find one small piece of evidence that would unlock everything.

While he was doing that, Recker and Haley went over to Vervaat's office. They went inside the building and up to the floor of Vervaat's office. The door was locked. There were a couple people walking through the hallway, but as soon as they disappeared, they worked on picking the lock. Recker stood watch as Haley got to work. He had it unlocked in almost no time.

They went in and started looking around. The secretary wasn't there. Vervaat's office was empty too. They started looking through everything they came across, hoping they would find some link to the case. Something that would springboard them onto whatever Vervaat's plans were next.

It was going to be a tall order, though. There wasn't much of the office left. The furniture and fixtures were all still there. But not much else. The secretary's desk was clear, with just the phone left on top of it. The drawers were empty.

Vervaat's office wasn't any different. There was a file cabinet, though there weren't any files. The desk was as clear as could be. And they couldn't find any papers lying around that would give them a clue as to what he was planning next.

"Looks like they left in a hurry," Haley said.

"Yeah. Not too much of a hurry, though. They didn't leave anything behind."

"No, but it sure does confirm that he's feeling the heat."

"Doesn't do us much good that he is."

"He'll trip up somewhere. They always do. Just have to be patient until he does."

"Hopefully that'll be sooner rather than later," Recker said.

"Check his house?"

"Not sure that'll be any different. But might as well."

They left the office and immediately drove over to Vervaat's house. He lived in a condo. End unit. Three floors. Nice place. There was no car in the driveway, though there was an attached garage. So they couldn't be positive that the man wasn't there. Recker and Haley stayed on the street for about half an hour, carefully looking at the house. But they didn't see any signs of movement inside. No lights turned on, they didn't notice a curtain shake, nothing.

Recker didn't believe the man was there. And he wasn't going to wait all day to prove it. They got out of their car and approached the house. They went straight for the back door. Back doors usually were less secure than the front door. And there was no fence around the property.

At this point, they weren't worried about getting picked up by cameras or any other security measures. Vervaat knew they were coming for him. They weren't worried if he saw them. Nothing was a secret by now.

As usual, it didn't take them long to get into the house. But just like Vervaat's office, there wasn't much there to analyze. While it wasn't completely cleaned out like the office was, there still wasn't much in the way of clues or information. The furniture was all still there. The kitchen cabinets and refrigerator were stocked. But after an exhaustive search of the place, they still came up empty.

There wasn't a piece of paper, a computer, a file folder, nothing was lying around that they could use to get information from. Nothing that would indicate what Vervaat's plans were, or where he was going. They appeared to hit a dead end. Not only was their chief suspect gone, he left without a trace.

"He left Dodge real quick," Haley said.

"Yeah. He was thorough about it, though."

"We'll pick him up. Either him or Sharma. One of them will make a mistake."

Recker didn't seem to share the enthusiasm of his partner. "We'll see."

Haley tapped his partner on the back, sensing his frustration. "And when we get the first one, he'll lead us to the other. Come on. Let's head back to the barn. No use in staying here any longer."

"Yeah. No use at all."

"If there's a good thing, I'd say we probably scared them out of town. Might not ever hear from them again."

Though it was extremely possible that was the case, Recker wasn't hoping so. That would feel like a loss to him. They were close to them, at least as far as knowing who was behind everything. He didn't want to lose the trail now. But unless something unforeseen happened, it didn't appear like he was going to get the shot he was hoping for.

28

A man was brought into the room. He was wearing a nice-looking brown suit. He had a hood over his face. The room was dark, only a small light hanging over the middle of the room. He had his hands tied behind his back. The man tried to talk, though his words were somewhat muffled under the black hood.

"What is going on?!"

Nobody responded to him. There were two other men in the room with him. One of them brought a chair into the middle of the room, while the other man pushed him down to sit on it. They then took off the hood.

The man squinted his eyes as he tried to adjust to his new surroundings. Considering the lack of light, it didn't take long. He looked around the room. There wasn't another piece of furniture in the small room. It was probably the size of a child's bedroom. But it was much colder than that. Not temperature wise. But the concrete floors and walls added to the ambience.

"What is going on here?! I demand to know the answer as to why I'm here!"

"Just hold on," an armed man said. "They'll be with you soon enough."

"Who's they?! Do you know who I am?! I will have your heads for this! Do you know who I am?!"

The door opened, with the man coming in acutely aware of who he was. Vincent knew everyone.

"Oh, I'm quite aware of who you are, Mr. Sharma."

Sharma's eyes almost bulged out. He was even more worried about his fate than he was before. He obviously knew Vincent on sight. Malloy was right behind his boss.

"What is the meaning of this?!" Sharma asked.

"I was under the impression that you wanted to meet with me. Is that not correct?"

Sharma instantly knew what he was referring to, though he obviously had to start thinking fast and coming up with a different story.

"I was just... I was just trying to gain an ally. That's all."

"It appears that plan has backfired," Vincent said.

"Why am I here?"

"It seems as if you have some answering to do."

"In regards to what? We have no business with each other."

"I would say that is an incorrect statement. I've heard your organization, as small as it already is, is already crumbling. It seems as if you have pissed off the wrong person."

"Nonsense. My organization is fine."

"Really? Then why did we find you attempting to board a train to Cleveland?"

"I had business there."

"More like attempting to flee the hot zone," Vincent replied.

"I don't see how any of this is your concern. My reasons, my actions, none of that is of any consequence to you."

"That's where you're incorrect. Everything that goes on here is my business. You and your partner, Mr. Vervaat, have been bringing down a ton of heat on the area. Diamond robberies are a big story. Especially when there are so many of them in a short span. And with the value of them? That's a big story. And it's only getting bigger."

"I don't know anything about that."

Vincent started laughing. "Do you know the worst thing you can do right about now? Lie to me. For a man in the position that you're in, that would be a terrible, terrible mistake. One might say... fatal. Isn't that right, Jimmy?"

Malloy cracked his knuckles. "Definitely."

"You see, not only have you incurred the wrath of The Silencer, but the police are on the alert, and even the FBI is out there, roaming around. And they're starting to poke their noses into things. Some of those things are my business. Things that have nothing to do with you or this diamond business. Now can you see why this is my concern?"

Sharma gulped. "Yes."

"Heat isn't good for business. It means I have to take things slowly, alter deals, or cancel them altogether while things are hot out there. Law enforcement is all over the city right now. And it's putting a dent into my plans."

"My sincerest apologies. It wasn't my idea."

"I'm sure it wasn't. You just saw a good opportunity and went along for the ride, right?"

"Something like that."

Vincent smiled. "You just did what any good businessman would do."

"Yes. That's right. But I'm done now. Like you said, it's getting too hot here. I'm leaving. You'll never have to worry about me again."

"Well, that would indicate that I ever worried about you to begin with. And that's obviously not the case."

Sharma already knew he was in deep trouble. But he couldn't shake the feeling that his troubles had only just begun. An eerie feeling was coming over him. The kind a person felt when danger was lurking. And it was lurking now.

"Anything you want me to do." He nervously smiled. And he was starting to sweat profusely. "Anything at all."

"I would like you to tell me where the diamonds are. And where I can find Damien Vervaat."

"I don't know that," Sharma replied.

He instantly felt a jolt across the side of his face, rocking him. He, along with his chair, tipped over onto the ground. The blow came courtesy of Malloy. Vincent's men picked Sharma and the chair up, putting it back in its original place.

"Those are words I do not like to hear," Vincent said. "Let me make myself perfectly clear. Nobody knows you're here. And the only way you're getting out of here is if I allow it."

"I swear I don't..."

"Before you finish that statement, let me tell you a story."

"I just..."

Vincent put his finger in the air to shush the man. "When I first heard about all this diamond business, I didn't think it concerned me much. I mean, a couple robberies, good for whoever was pulling them off. It didn't affect me much. But then, they kept happening. It got The Silencer on the trail. It brought heat. More heat than I would prefer. Bodies start dropping. The heat intensifies. Things are happening."

"I swear I..."

Vincent one again put his finger in the air to quiet his guest. "So I say to myself, 'what can I do to alleviate all this'? And you know what I came up with?"

Sharma shook his head.

Vincent smirked. "By handling it myself. I put feelers out, put my contacts to work, get my sources in order, and I scour the area. The best way to stomp this into the ground is by eliminating the problem personally. Then my problems go away. That makes sense, doesn't it?"

Sharma nodded.

"So for me, from my perspective, what helps me... is this business going away. The Silencer goes back to doing his thing. The police go back to doing their thing. The FBI goes on their way. The diamonds are returned like nothing ever happened. And everybody's happy. Everybody wins. Doesn't that sound like the best way of going about this?"

Sharma nodded again. It may have been a dark, and cold room, but he was sure feeling the heat. Vincent just had a way of talking that made it seem like a person was about to be buried any minute.

"Now, you're in this up to your neck. So don't try and tell me otherwise. You know what's going on."

"I just..."

Vincent once again put his finger up. He wasn't interested in hearing a rebuttal. He was only interested in saying what he had to say. And he wasn't done yet.

"I like to think I'm a fair man. Tough. But fair. So in the interest of fairness, I'd like to offer you a deal. One that I don't think you're worth. One that I don't think you deserve. But one I'm prepared to offer anyway. Are you interested?"

Sharma looked a little dubious, but was nevertheless intrigued. "What kind of deal?"

"You tell me everything you know about this. The crew used to pull off the robberies. Where the diamonds currently are. And where we can find Damien Vervaat."

"And if I do?"

"Well, I could threaten you with death," Vincent said with a laugh. "But I won't go that far. At least, not right now. First, I'll offer you a proposal."

"What kind of proposal?"

"If you're honest, and tell me everything you know, I'll set you up somewhere else. Somewhere far away. But I'll set you up with a good stake, I'll offer my guidance, and in return I'll take a portion of your profits. But I can make you the top dog in some other city. That's as good of an offer as you'll ever get."

Sharma could hardly believe it. This was a golden opportunity. One he couldn't believe was being offered. This was all working out even more perfectly than he could have ever imagined.

"Seriously? You'll do that?"

Vincent nodded. "Absolutely. But I need this other business behind me. As I said, I don't care about it for any other reason except that it's crippling my plans for other activities."

That was all Sharma needed to hear. "OK. OK, yeah. I can do that."

"So we have a deal?"

"Yes. Yes, absolutely."

Vincent smiled. "Jimmy. Untie our new partner here. We have things to discuss."

Sharma smiled, suddenly feeling upbeat about his situation.

"I apologize for the rougher treatment you've received so far. But it had to be done to ensure your understanding of the situation."

"Oh, no, I understand," Sharma happily replied. "I would've done the same thing in your situation."

Vincent grinned. Everything was going exactly as he hoped it would.

"Now, tell me everything you know."

After Sharma spilled his guts and told Vincent everything he knew, which was quite a bit, the crime boss was satisfied that Sharma was being truthful. It didn't sound like a man making stuff up and throwing things at the wall to see what stuck. Vincent then motioned for his trusted lieutenant to follow him out of the room to have some privacy.

"What do you think?" Vincent asked.

"Sounded believable to me."

"I agree."

"What do you want to do now?" Malloy asked.

"Let's do a little follow up, and then we'll turn over what we've learned to our Silencer friends."

"What about Sharma? Where are we going to send him?"

Vincent glared at him, almost a gleam in his eye. "Oh, you know where to send him."

29

Recker and Haley arrived at the office almost at the same time, getting there only a minute apart. They met each other in the parking lot, then walked in together. After walking in, they were greeted by a look on Jones' face that indicated something major went down. He always had that certain look on him when he was in the know.

"Why do you look like that?" Recker asked.

"I take it you haven't heard?"

"Heard what?"

"I'll assume that's a no," Jones replied. "Otherwise you wouldn't need to ask."

"Heard what?"

Jones didn't respond. He simply grabbed the remote off the desk and turned on the TV on the wall. The news came on. Jones had recorded the section that was interesting so he could play it back in its entirety for his partners. A reporter was on the screen, in front of a crime scene, as obvious as it was with the yellow caution tape and police presence around. She was next to a building, though it wasn't immediately clear which one it was. Jones turned up the volume so they could hear what was being reported.

"The body of Kavi Sharma was found just a few hours ago in this alley here behind me. There is no word yet as far as a suspect or motive, but I have learned that foul play is suspected, as the victim was found under a few trash bags by a dumpster, and he had three bullet holes in his chest. He was pronounced DOA when the police were notified and arrived. It should be noted that Sharma is reported to have criminal ties, though police say it is too early to determine whether this is some kind of gangland hit, or whether Sharma was just in the wrong place, at the wrong time. Back to you, Greg."

Recker continued staring at the screen for a minute, long after the reporter had finished her story, and the news continued on to another topic. He wasn't sure what to make of it at first. He finally turned his head to look at Haley.

"What do you make of that?" Haley asked.

"A falling out between him and Vervaat?" Jones said. "They were obviously in bed together. Must have had a disagreement."

"A fatal one."

Recker wasn't so sure. It certainly seemed plausible, though he questioned the timing of it.

"Why?" Recker asked.

"Maybe Vervaat thought Sharma was dead weight," Haley answered. "Not holding up his end of the bargain."

"Yes, especially after what you two did at his office," Jones said. "Maybe it was felt that Sharma was no longer useful. Or capable."

"Always possible," Recker replied.

"Or maybe it was thought that Sharma was starting to buckle under the weight of the pressure we've been putting on."

There was still something nagging Recker about it, though. It just didn't feel like something Vervaat would do. He wasn't known as the especially violent sort. And three bullet holes to the chest and left under some trash bags in the back of an alley didn't seem like the type of move someone like Vervaat would make.

"What's bothering you about it?" Jones asked. "I can tell something is."

"Does this seem like something Vervaat would do?"

"Why wouldn't it? Could be a thousand reasons for it. Falling out, don't trust him, keep more of the money, I could go on and on."

"Yeah, but the way it was done seems especially cold and violent. Three bullet holes, under trash bags, in an alley, late at night. None of that screams Vervaat to me. I could see Vervaat doing it, but in a different manner."

Jones didn't see what the problem was in any event. "Even if it was someone else, what difference does it make?"

"Maybe there's another player involved."

Jones shook his head. He didn't buy it. "We've only got one player left. Damien Vervaat. Why are you trying to make something more out of it than what it is?"

"I'm not trying to make more out of it," Recker said. "I'm just trying to make sense out of it."

"As far as I can tell, we've got one less worry than we did yesterday," Haley said. "Doesn't really matter how or why it happened."

"Agreed," Jones responded. "Now our attention does not have to be split and we can focus all of our efforts on one man instead of two."

In the end, Recker reluctantly agreed with his partners. The particulars didn't really matter. All that mattered was that they no longer had to worry about Sharma. And Vervaat was the only target they had left. They all went to work on trying to locate where Vervaat was at the moment. He was on the run, with his office and home no longer options to find him.

After about an hour, Recker's phone rang. It was Malloy. Considering what they already learned today, Malloy calling raised Recker's antenna.

"Hey, heard the big news?" Recker asked.

"What big news?"

"Kavi Sharma. He was found dead this morning."

"No kidding?"

"You didn't know anything about it?"

"No, first I've heard," Malloy answered. "How about that? It's kind of funny how that works, though."

"Yeah? How's that?"

"Here I was calling to talk to you about all that diamond business, and you're breaking news to me at the same time, about the same thing."

"Yeah. Funny. What news did you have?"

"I got a source who's pretty connected who claims to know where Vervaat is. He's the guy you're looking for, right?"

"That's right. How would this guy know?"

"He's got his ways. Maybe a little birdie told him."

"And you believe this guy?" Recker asked.

"I do. Seemed to know quite a bit of inside stuff. Knew about the robberies, Vervaat, how Sharma was involved, the crew involved, all of it. And he knew about where the diamonds were heading."

"Which is?"

"On the way to Europe next week. Big shipment. Already has a buyer lined up. Vervaat's just laying low until then."

"Where is he?"

"Secluded cabin. In the Pocono's."

Recker was still dubious about how all this information was known. "You don't happen to know the address, do you?"

"Of course I do."

"It's a little strange that you happen to get all this information the same day that Sharma is found dead."

"Coincidence," Malloy replied.

"You know how I feel about those."

"Sometimes it happens."

"Jimmy, be straight with me. Are you guys responsible for Sharma?"

"Mike, why do you ask questions you really don't want the answers to? Just be happy that you're getting what you want. That's all that really matters, right?"

"I suppose so." Recker knew what was going on now. But he still had questions. And he did want the answers. "Theoretically speaking... if someone had all this information, why wouldn't they just go there themselves, take the diamonds, sell them, do what they want. Why get me involved?"

"Well, since I don't know all the particulars, I can only make an educated guess."

"Be interested to hear your take on it."

"I would assume the diamonds aren't of interest to whoever found this out. It's what, a few hundred thousand? Something like that? Wouldn't really make much of a dent into a bigger operation."

"That's all there is to it?"

"Maybe all these robberies are bringing too much publicity to the area. Cramping plans."

Now Recker knew what the deal was. He understood.

"So whoever got this information just basically wants all of this to go away. Like nothing ever happened."

"That's what I would assume," Malloy said. "But I'm not in the know. Just guessing."

"Oh, of course, of course. It's good to bounce these ideas off you, though. Speaking of all of this, you don't happen to know what Vervaat's situation is up there, do you? How many men, security, all that?"

"From what I understand, he's got the three members of the crew with him for protection."

"That's it?" Recker asked.

"That's my understanding. Whether he's recruited anymore today or anything, I can't say."

"All right, thanks. I appreciate it."

"No problem. What are friends for, right?"

"I guess Vincent won't be sad to hear the news about Sharma, huh? One more guy he won't have to worry about."

"He was never worried about him. But... he sure won't be sad about it. And hey, depending on when you embark on this trip, let me know if you need a little extra help. Be glad to go up there with you. Or send a few of the boys."

"I'll have to get back to you on that."

"No problem. Let me know."

Recker hung up and instantly looked at both of his

partners. They were both staring at him. Overhearing part of the conversation, they could sense something big was up. Recker then got a text message confirming the address of where Vervaat was staying.

"Looks like we hit the jackpot," Recker said.

"Vervaat?" Haley asked.

Recker nodded. "Signed, sealed, and delivered."

"Vincent?" Jones said.

"They apparently heard it from a 'source'," Recker said, putting it in air quotes.

Haley laughed. "That's a good one."

"Anyway, I guess it doesn't really matter how we have it. We just have it."

"He's dead?"

"No. He's hiding out with the three members of his crew. Holding out until next week when they're off to Europe to unload the diamonds."

"We know where?"

Recker nodded. "We do. Looks like we're heading to the mountains."

30

Before leaving for the Pocono's, the team constructed a plan on how they were going to operate. They didn't really want to be leaving a trail of bodies in their wake. After looking up the address that Malloy gave them, the house Vervaat was staying in would play into their hands perfectly. The house was situated on a few acres, and was on the lake. There were options.

None of those options included barging straight in and taking out whoever was in their path. Though it was a hunting area, and hearing a gunshot didn't alarm most people, they would be going in after dark. They wanted to work this quietly.

In order to pull off what they wanted, they figured they'd need some help. Malloy was only too happy to lend his services. He, and one more of Vincent's men, embarked with them on their trip.

They waited until midnight struck. It was a dark night. The moon was covered. The conditions were perfect.

Figuring that if Vervaat and his men were watching, which was pretty much a given, going through the front didn't seem like the best option for being undetected. That obviously left the back. Considering the house was on the lake, Vervaat probably didn't think too much about the lack of security back there. But that was where Recker would enter.

Malloy was able to grab a small boat, entering from the other end of the lake. They headed straight for Vervaat's place, though they cut the engine once they got somewhat near it to disguise their movements. It wasn't a big boat, but it was enough to hold about ten people with room to spare.

Recker and Haley were on the edge of the boat, in their gear, ready to drop into the water once they got closer to the house.

"Been a while since I did this," Haley said. "Brings back some memories."

"Yeah. This should be one of the easier jobs, though," Recker replied. "The last time I had to move in on a target from the water when I was with the agency, there were fifteen targets that needed to be disposed of."

"Nothing like good odds. How'd you make it with it?"

"Piece of cake."

As they drifted toward the house, Malloy came over to them.

"You sure this is how you guys wanna do this?"

"It's for the best," Recker answered.

"I mean, why get all wet when we can just barge through the front?"

"They're gonna have someone watching. And I don't really wanna advertise our presence."

"Yeah, I guess. Just seems like a lot of extra work."

"It's not always about doing it the fastest way," Recker said. "We were taught a long time ago that the fastest way isn't always the best way. The best way is however you can get the job done without anyone knowing you were ever there. If that takes a longer path, or more time, then that's what it takes."

Haley agreed with the assessment. "If you go in the front guns blazing, everyone and their mother will know something happened here. Brings a lot of scrutiny. But if you do it this way, it's like nothing ever happened."

Malloy scratched the side of his head. "I can't argue the logic. Just... I dunno. Guess it's not my style."

"We know," Recker said. "We'll take care of it. Just make sure you get this boat near the shore by the time we're ready to leave."

"It'll be there."

After a few more minutes, Recker and Haley dropped into the water, and swam toward the shore. Once they got there, they crawled onto a small sandy area, taking some of their gear off along the way. They remained stationary for a minute, sizing up what they were looking at.

The back of the house was dark. There were no outside lights on. But they could see that a couple of rooms inside the house did have lights on. They were secretly hoping that all of them would be sitting outside, huddled around a campfire, drinking themselves into a stupor. But unfortunately that wasn't the case. They'd actually have to work a little harder than that.

Using the plentiful trees and bushes that were in the area as cover, Recker and Haley slowly made their move toward the house. They were going a little slow, but they had the time. And there was no need to rush.

Within a few minutes, they finally got near the house. They were just about to make their move when a door suddenly opened up. A man came out. He said something to someone who must've been inside, though they couldn't make out what it was, and walked out, stretching his arms. He yawned. As he did, they could see a pistol attached to his side.

Recker sent some hand signals Haley's way to let him know what he wanted to do. He didn't want this guy dead. At least, not yet. They could use this guy to let them know how many people they'd be dealing with.

The man walked down to the edge of the water and looked at the lake for a few minutes. As he turned around to walk back to the house, Haley intentionally stepped on some leaves and branches. He wanted the guy's attention. With the darkness, the man couldn't see what it was. But he heard it. He pulled his gun out and started walking toward where the noises were coming from.

As the man got closer, Haley made a few more noises with his feet. The man was a little startled, hearing it so close. He still couldn't see Haley, though. As soon as he passed a tree, he felt a hard thump on the top of his head, courtesy of Recker's weapon. The man instantly dropped to the ground.

The man was dazed, and moaned and groaned as he moved around on the ground. By the time he got his wits about him again, his eyes opened wide as he saw the two guns pointed straight at his head.

"Tell us what we want to know and you'll live," Recker said. "Lie and you're dead. Simple as that. Two choices. And be quiet about it. Which is it?"

It wasn't much of a choice for the man. "What do you want?"

"How many people inside?"

"Five including me."

"All armed?"

The man nodded.

"You the guys that were doing all the diamond robberies?" Recker asked.

"Yeah."

"Vervaat behind it all?"

"It was his idea."

"Is he inside?"

"Yes."

"Where are the diamonds?"

"Inside in a safe."

"You know the combination?"

"Only Damien does."

"So there's four other people we gotta deal with?" Recker asked.

"Yes."

"Where are they?"

"All spread out. I'm not sure now."

"Fine. You did good. Turn over and put your hands behind your back."

The man was obviously worried. "What are you gonna do?"

"You did good. We're just gonna tie your hands together. We're gonna leave you alone here for a minute. Once we leave, you get up, and walk down to the lake. They'll be a boat there to pick you up. If you decide to walk back to the house, you're gonna get shot. Understand?"

"I got it."

Recker and Haley left the man there, then proceeded to go back near the house, using the trees once again as cover.

"You sure that was a good idea leaving him there?" Haley asked.

"There's not much he'll be able to do. If he comes back, he knows he's dead."

"He could just escape through the woods."

Recker shrugged, not really caring about it. "Still gets him out of our hair one way or another. As long as we don't have to worry about him, it doesn't matter which path he chooses."

Recker and Haley then darted toward the house, getting there without incident. They stood to the side of the door that the other man came out of and opened it. They didn't just want to barge in. Then they heard a voice.

"Are you coming in or what?!"

A man came to the door and looked out. As soon as he saw the intruders, he went for his gun. Considering Recker already had his out, it wasn't much of a contest. And the silencer on the end of Recker's weapon muffled the sound.

Now Recker and Haley rushed into the house, immediately splitting up as they took different rooms upon entry. There was one man sitting on a couch watching TV. As soon as he saw Recker, he jumped up, though he was so surprised, he was fumbling around with his gun, unable to properly pick it up off the couch he was sitting on. Recker put him down quite easily.

Haley found another man in the kitchen. He was just sitting at the table, a bottle of whiskey in front of him, and a glass that was mostly empty. His gun was next to the bottle. Once he saw Haley, he reached for it, though it was too late, as Haley blasted him off his seat.

The rest of the house was empty except for one. Damien Vervaat. Recker and Haley went room by room until they found their man. Vervaat was in a bedroom, though it also doubled as an office. There was a bed, a desk, a small file cabinet, along with the usual bedroom furniture.

As soon as Vervaat saw the two men, he raced across the room, hoping to reach the gun he had in one of the desk drawers. He didn't make it even halfway, though.

"Not even worth trying," Recker said.

Vervaat came to a halt, knowing it was a fruitless effort. He halfheartedly put his arms up, though they barely made it past his waist.

"What do you guys want?"

Recker cracked a smile. "Seriously? You really have to ask?"

"I really don't know."

"The diamonds, stupid."

"What diamonds."

"We should shoot him just for being stupid," Haley said.

"All your buddies are dead," Recker said. "There's no help coming for you. And you have no other play here."

Vervaat cleared his throat as he tried to think of some options. He really didn't have any. Except for one.

Recker's eyes glanced around the room. He didn't see what he was looking for.

"Where's the safe?"

"What safe?" Vervaat asked.

"One more dumb answer and you're gonna lose a leg. You understand that?"

Vervaat nodded. "Perfectly."

"I'm really not the type of guy you wanna play games with. Where's the safe? I promise you I won't ask again."

Vervaat didn't really want to get shot. And he believed Recker would do it if he kept pushing his buttons. "Under the desk."

"Under the desk?"

"Floor safe."

"Get to cracking," Recker said.

"Why? What do you hope to find?"

Recker slightly shook his head, hardly believing the stupidity of the question. "The diamonds."

"I already sold them."

"OK. We'll just see what else you got in there, then."

Vervaat sighed. He could see there was nothing he could say or do other than what the men wanted. He slowly walked over to the desk and started to move it. As he pulled it over, Recker could see the floor safe.

Vervaat got down on one knee and started to spin the dial. He unlocked it. But he didn't open it yet.

Instead, he had one last plea. An offer that he hoped the men would accept.

"How about we make a deal?"

"How about we don't," Recker answered.

"No, really. Two hundred thousand dollars for each of you. That's a pretty good haul."

"Not interested."

"What do you want, then?"

"Just the diamonds."

"If I give them to you, you'll let me leave."

"Not a chance. You're going to jail."

"I can't do that."

"You don't have a choice. You're going."

Vervaat took a deep breath. He opened the safe. He then reached into it.

"Make sure you don't do anything stupid while you're in there," Recker said.

Vervaat slowly pulled out a small black bag. He lifted it up high, and Haley came over and took it. Haley took a step back and opened it.

"Is that it?" Recker asked.

"No, there's another," Vervaat said. He pulled out another bag, also handing it to Haley. "That should do it."

"Stand up."

As Haley took a step back to show his partner, Vervaat quickly jumped up, holding a gun in his hand that he pulled from the safe. Recker already had his gun on him, though. This was a trick he'd seen too many times. It rarely worked. He didn't figure Vervaat was going to go down without a fight.

But with three bullet wounds to his chest, Vervaat went down just the same. With him dead, Haley went over to the safe and checked it. He saw another bag in there and took it out.

"I guess this'll do it," Haley said.

"Yeah. Guess so."

With the situation now under control, and the diamonds in hand, they started cleaning up. They weren't leaving any dead bodies there to be discovered. They started dragging all of the bodies down to the edge of the lake, where Malloy's boat was now in full view, just waiting there for them.

With Malloy's help, they put all of the bodies onto the boat. Before leaving, Recker and Malloy cleaned up any blood that was on the floor inside. It wasn't a perfect job. But it was good enough for their purposes. Then they rejoined Malloy on the boat, along with the dead bodies that needed to be disposed of.

"What do you plan on doing with them?" Haley asked.

"I dunno," Malloy replied. "Maybe we'll put them in the concrete of a new building being constructed. Or there's always dumping them here in the lake."

"Bodies dumped in water always have a habit of turning up somewhere," Recker replied.

"You're right. Concrete, it is. Get all the diamonds that were stolen?"

Recker took out one of the bags and put some of the diamonds in his hand. "I assume this is most, if not all of them."

"Sure do look nice."

"Yeah. They sure do."

As Recker put the diamonds away again, Malloy started the boat, and they began moving. The clouds started moving, letting the light of the moon shine down. Malloy laughed.

"There's the moon. Right on cue."

"Almost like it was waiting for us to finish up," Haley replied.

"Hey, that almost looked like fun. Dropping into the water and getting up on the house like that. Maybe next time you'll let me tag along."

Recker looked at Malloy for a moment as they sped away. Malloy had joined them in quite a few jobs over the years, it was almost like a third member of the team. Very often, he didn't even need to be there. He just volunteered. It didn't go unnoticed.

Recker knew his days wouldn't go on forever. At some point, he would walk away. And though they tried an addition with Phillips, which obviously didn't work, they'd eventually try again. Probably. And who better to try it with than someone who was already familiar with them.

Though there were obviously some tendencies that Malloy would have to break or adjust, Recker knew it was in him to do that. Of course, there was the whole

Vincent problem, which was a big problem that would have to be dealt with.

"Have you ever thought about...?" Recker didn't finish his thought. He figured now wasn't the time.

"What?" Malloy asked.

"Nevermind. It's not important. There'll be time for it later."

"What's that?"

"Just a... something I was thinking about. Actually, I have to do some more thinking about it."

"OK. You let me know when you're ready to talk about it, huh?"

Recker nodded. "I will. Somewhere further up the line. But I'll let you know. I'll let you know."

ALSO BY MIKE RYAN

Continue reading the The Silencer Series with the next book, Death Watch

Other works:

The Nate Thrower Series

The Extractor Series

The Eliminator Series

The Cari Porter Series

The Cain Series

The Ghost Series

The Brandon Hall Series

A Dangerous Man

The Last Job

The Crew

ABOUT THE AUTHOR

Mike Ryan is a USA Today Bestselling Author, and lives in Pennsylvania with his wife, and four children. He's the author of numerous bestselling books. Visit his website at www.mikeryanbooks.com to find out more about his books, and sign up for his newsletter, where you will get exclusive short stories, and never miss a release date. You can also interact with Mike via Facebook, and Instagram.

       facebook.com/mikeryanauthor
       instagram.com/mikeryanauthor